Provocative

That was how she looked. A fine, sleek creature of sensual provocation.

Not that she was aware of any of this, he acknowledged grimly.

Unaware. Just as she was of the fact that her wedding ring gleamed gold on her finger.

His wedding ring. The ring he had placed there. Once a gold ring of love, now a gold ring of betrayal.

MICHELLE REID grew up on the southern edges of Manchester, England, the youngest in a family of five lively children. But now she lives in the beautiful county of Cheshire with her busy executive husband and two grown-up daughters. She loves reading, the ballet and playing tennis when she gets the chance. She hates cooking, cleaning, and despises ironing! Sleep she can do without, and she produces some of her best written work during the early hours of the morning.

Michelle Reid

Gold Ring of Betrayal

Harlequin Books

TORONTO • NEW YORK • LONDON
AMSTERDAM • PARIS • SYDNEY • HAMBURG
STOCKHOLM • ATHENS • TOKYO • MILAN
MADRID • WARSAW • BUDAPEST • AUCKLAND

ISBN 0-373-11917-8

GOLD RING OF BETRAYAL

First North American Publication 1997.

CHAPTER ONE

LONDON. Big house. Big address close to Hyde Park. The time: 17.45 p.m. Six hours since it happened.

And the tension in the formal drawing room was so fraught it picked at the flesh. People were standing about in small clusters, some talking in low, worried voices, some breaking into soft bouts of weeping now and then, others comforting, others holding themselves apart from it all, standing or sitting with a fierce self-control about them which held them silent and still.

Waiting.

Sara was of the latter group, sitting alone on one of the soft-cushioned sofas. She appeared calm, outwardly composed now as she stared down at the pale carpet beneath her feet, seemingly oblivious to everyone else.

But she was far from oblivious. Far from composed. Every movement, each sound was reverberating shrilly inside her head. And she was sitting there like that, straight-backed and very still, because she knew that if she did so much as move a muscle all her severely reined in self-control would gush screaming out of her.

It had already happened once. When the dreadful news had been brought to her, her initial reaction had been one of almost uncontrollable horror. They had tried to put her to bed then. Tried to force tranquillizers down her throat to put her out of her torment. Tried to render her oblivious to it all.

She'd refused. Of course she'd refused! How could any woman—any mother take refuge in sleep at a time like this?

But because they had been alarmed by her reaction, because they'd needed something tangible to worry about and she'd seemed the most obvious candidate, and because she'd found she did not have it in her to fight them as well as fight the multitude of terrors rattling around inside her head she had made herself calm down, pretend to get a hold on herself, and had taken up her silent vigil here, on this sofa, where she had been sitting for hours now. Hours . . .

Waiting.

Like the rest of them. Waiting for the man who was at the centre of all this trauma to come and take control of the situation.

He was on his way, they'd told her, as though expecting that piece of information to make her feel better. It didn't. Nothing did. Nothing would.

So she sat very still, blue eyes lowered so no one could see what was happening inside her head, and concentrated all her attention on remaining calm while they, in their own anxiety, did not seem to notice the way the stark blackness of her long-sleeved T-shirt and tight leggings accentuated the whitened strain in her face. Nor did they seem to realise that she was sitting so straight because shock was holding her spine like a rigid rod of iron, or that her hands, clasped quietly on her lap, were in actual fact clenched and cold and so stiff that she didn't think she could unclasp them again even if she tried to.

But at least they didn't approach. At least they weren't trying to comfort her by murmuring useless platitudes no mother wanted to hear at a time like this. At least they were leaving her alone.

The sudden sound of crunching tyres on the gravel driveway outside the house had everyone else jumping to attention. Sara did not move. She did not so much as lift her head in response.

There was the sound of voices in the hallway, one deep, sharp and authoritative, standing out from the rest as special. And the air in the room began to fizz.

Then footsteps, firm, precise, came towards the closed drawing-room door. Everyone inside the room turned towards it as it shot open, their eyes fixing expectantly on the man who appeared in its aperture.

But Sara kept her gaze fixed on the small square of carpet she'd had it fixed on for ages now, carefully counting the tiny rosebuds which made up part of the pale blue and peach design.

Tall, lean-featured, black hair, tight body. White shirt, dark tie, grey suit that sat on him as expensive silk should. Tanned skin—natural, not worked on. Long, thin nose, ruthlessly drawn, resolute sensual mouth. And the sharp and shrewd eyes of a hunter. Gold, like a tiger. Cold, like the features. A man hewn from rock.

He stood poised like that in the doorway for some long, immeasurable seconds, emitting a leashed power into the room that had everyone else holding their breath. His strange eyes flicked from one anxious face to another, surveying the scene as a whole without so much as acknowledging a single person. The young girl sitting in a chair by the window let out a muffled sob when his gaze touched her; her cheeks blotchy, eyes red and swollen, she stared up at him as if she were begging for her very life. Coldly, dismissively he moved on—and on. Until his eyes found Sara, sitting there in her isolated splendour, face lowered and seemingly unaware.

Then something happened to the eyes. What was difficult to determine but it sent an icy chill down the spines of those who saw it. He began to move, loose-limbed and graceful. Without so much as affording anyone else a second glance he walked across the patterned carpet and came to a stop directly in front of her.

'Sara,' he prompted quietly.

She did not move. Her eyes did focus dimly on the pair of handmade leather shoes which were now obscuring the patch of carpet she had been concentrating on. But other than that she showed no sign that she was aware of his presence.

'Sara.' There was more command threaded into the tone this time.

It had the required effect, making her dusky lashes quiver before her eyes began the slow, sluggish journey upwards, skimming his long, silk-clad legs, powerful thighs, his lean, tight torso made of solid muscle and covered by a white shirt that did not quite manage to hide the abundance of crisp black hair shadowing satin-smooth, stretched-leather skin beneath.

She reached the throat, taut and tanned. Then the chin, rigidly chiselled. Then the shadow of a line that was his grimly held, perfectly sculptured mouth. His nose thin, straight and uncompromisingly masculine. Cheeks, lean and sheened with the silken lustre of well cared for skin. Then at last the eyes. Her blank blue gaze lifted to clash with the hunter's gold eyes belonging to the one man in this world whom she had most wished never to see again.

What was it? she found herself thinking dully. Two years since she'd seen him—coming closer to three? He had changed little.

Yet why should he have changed? He was Nicolas Santino. Big man. Powerful man. A wealthy man who could afford houses with big addresses in every important capital of the world. He was a slick, smooth, beautifully cared for human being. Born to power, raised to power and used to power. When he frowned people cowered.

The man with everything. Good looks, great body. Why should three small years change any of that? He possessed the godlike features of a man of fable. The hair, so black it gleamed navy blue in the light. The nose, that arrogant appendage he made no apologies for. The mouth, firm, set, a perfectly drawn shadow on a golden bone structure hewn from the same privileged rock those fabled men had come from. And finally the eyes. The eyes of a lion, a tiger, a sleek black panther.

The eyes of a hard, cold, ruthless predator. Cruel and unforgiving.

Unforgiving.

If her mouth had been up to it, it would have smiled, albeit bitterly.

He the unforgiving one. She the sinner.

It was a shame she viewed the whole situation the other way around. It meant that neither was prepared to give an inch. Or hate the other less.

Three years, she was thinking. Three years of cold, silent festering. And it was all still there—lying hidden beneath the surface right now, but there all the same. Three years since he had last allowed himself to share the same space as her. And now he had the gall to appear before her and say her name as though it were the most natural thing in the world for him to do.

But it wasn't. And they both knew it wasn't. And Sara was in no fit state to play stupid, pride-saving games to the opposite. Not with him. Not with this man, whom she had once loved and now hated with the same intensity.

She looked away, eyes lowering back down his length, dismissing his handsome face, dismissing his superb body, dismissing his long legs encased in expensive silk. Dismissing the man in his entirety.

The message was loud and clear. The room gasped.

'Get out.'

It was quietly spoken, almost conversationally so, yet there was not a person in the room who did not understand the command or whom it was aimed directly at. Indifferent to them all, unmoving, he remained directly in front of Sara's bowed head while he waited in silence for his instruction to be carried out.

And they jolted into action, responding like mechanical toys, heads, bodies, limbs jerking with a complete lack of coordination that shifted them *en masse* towards the door. Two policemen, both in plain clothes. One uniformed chauffeur, hat gone, hair mussed, face white. One weepy young nanny with her face buried in a handkerchief. A harried-looking housekeeper and her grim-faced man-of-all-trades husband. And the doctor who had been called out to treat the young nanny and had ended up staying because he had been seriously concerned that Sara was ready to collapse.

Or maybe because he had been ordered to stay by this man.

Who knew—who cared? Sara didn't. He might be able to make other people quail in their shoes. He might be able to command mute obedience from anyone who came within his despotic reach. But not her. Never her! And she found it amazing if not pathetic that one man could walk in somewhere and command that kind of sheep-like obedience without even having to give his name.

But then, this one man was not just any man. This was a man who wielded such power that he could walk into any room anywhere in the world and command im-mediate attention. The same man who had had this house and its beautiful grounds locked up like a fortress within an hour of the incident happening.

It was a shame he had not had the foresight to do it before it had happened. Then this unwelcome meeting between them would not have needed to take place.

The last one out drew the door shut behind them. Sara heard it close with a gentle click, and felt the new silence settle around her like a shroud.

He moved away, coming back moments later to sit down beside her. The next thing, a glass was being pressed to her bloodless mouth.

'Drink,' he commanded.

The distinctive smell of brandy invading her nostrils almost made her gag and she shook her head, her waist-length, fine-spun, straight golden hair shimmering against her black-clad shoulders and arms.

He ignored the gesture. 'Drink,' he repeated. 'You look like death,' he added bluntly. 'Drink or I shall make you.'

No idle threat. That became clear when his hand came up, his long, strong, blunt-ended fingers taking a grip on her chin so he could force her mouth open.

She drank—then gasped as the liquid slid like fire down her paper-dry throat, the air sucking frantically into her lungs as though it had been trying to do that for hours now without any success.

'That's better,' he murmured, believing it was the brandy that had made her gasp like that when in actual fact it had been his touch—his touch acting like an electric charge to her system, shooting stinging shocks of recognition into every corner of her frozen flesh. 'Now drink some more.'

She drank, if only to hide the new horror that was attacking her. Him. This man. The bitter fact that she could still respond so violently to physical contact with this—person who had caused her so much pain and disillusionment and grief.

He made her take several sips at the brandy before deciding she'd had enough. His fingers let go. The glass was removed. By then the brandy had put some colour back into her cheeks—and his touch a glint of bitter condemnation into the blue eyes she managed to lift to his.

'Is this your doing?' she demanded, the words barely distinguishable as they scraped across her tense throat.

But he heard—and understood. The hardening of the eyes told her so. Eyes that continued to view her with a cold but steady scrutiny which quite efficiently gave her a reply.

He was denying it, using his eyes to demand how she dared suspect him of such a terrible thing.

But she did suspect him. 'I hate you,' she said. 'I despise the very ground you occupy. If anything happens to my baby then watch your back, Nicolas,' she warned him. 'Because I'll be there with a knife long enough to slice right through that piece of cold rock you may call a heart.'

He didn't respond, didn't react, which came as a surprise because his overgrown sense of self did not take kindly to threats. And she'd meant it—every single huskily spoken, virulent word.

'Tell me what happened,' he instructed quietly instead.

Her mind went hot at the bright, burning flashback to the young nanny stumbling through the door. 'Lia has been kidnapped!' she had screamed in outright hysteria. 'They just ran up and snatched her while we were playing in the park!'

The memory launched her from a wax-like dummy into a shivering, shaking mass of anguish. 'You *know* what happened, you evil monster!' she seared at him. Blue eyes sparked down on him with hatred, with fear, with a bitter, filthy contempt. 'She was your one humiliation so you've had her removed, haven't you—*haven't you?*'

By contrast the golden eyes remained calm, unaffected. He sat back, crossed one neat ankle over a beautifully clad knee, stretched a silk-clad arm across the back of the sofa and studied her quivering frame quite detachedly.

'I did not take your child,' he stated.

Not *his* child, she noted. Not even *our* child. Her shaking mouth compressed into a line of disgust. 'Yes, you did.' She said it without a hint of uncertainty. 'It bears all the hallmarks of one of your lot.' Not said nicely and not meant to be. 'Vendetta is your middle name. Or should be. The only thing I don't understand is why I wasn't taken out at the same time.'

'Work on it,' he suggested. 'You may, with a bit of luck, come up with a half-intelligent answer.'

She turned away, hating to look at him, hating that look of cruel indifference on his arrogant face. This was their daughter's life they were discussing here! And he could sit there looking like—that!

'God, you make me sick,' she breathed, moving away, arms wrapping around her tense body as she went to stand by the window, gazing out on the veritable wall of security now cordoning off the property: men with mobile telephones fastened to their ears, some with big, ugly-looking dogs on strong-looking leashes. A laugh broke from her, thick with scorn. 'Putting on a show for the punters,' she derided. 'Do you honestly think anyone will be fooled by it?'

'Not you, obviously!' He didn't even try to misunderstand what she was talking about, his mockery as dry as her derision. 'They are there to keep the media at bay,' he then flatly explained. 'That foolish nanny was supposed to be trained on how to respond to this kind of contingency. Instead she stood in the park screaming so loud that she brought half of London out to find out what was the matter.' His sigh showed the first hint of anger. 'Now the whole world knows that the child has been taken. Which is going to really make it simple to get her back with the minimum of fuss!'

'Oh, God.' Sara's hand went up to cover her mouth, panic suddenly clawing at her again. 'Why, Nicolas?' she cried in wretched despair. 'She's only two years old! She was no threat to you! Why did you take my baby away?'

She didn't see him move, yet he was at her side in an instant, his fingers burning that damned electrical charge into her flesh as he spun her around to face him. 'I won't repeat this again,' he clipped. 'So listen well. I did not take your child.'

'S-someone did,' she choked, blue eyes luminous with bulging tears. 'Who else do you know who hated her enough to do that?'

He sighed again, not answering that one—not answering because he couldn't deny her accusation. 'Come and sit down again before you drop,' he suggested. 'And we will—'

'I don't want to sit down!' she angrily refused. 'And I don't want you touching me!' Violently, she wrenched free of his grasp.

His mouth tightened, a sign that at last her manner towards him was beginning to get through his thick skin. 'Who else, Nicolas?' she repeated starkly. 'Who else would want to take my baby from me?'

'Not from *you*,' he said quietly, turning away. 'They have taken her from *me*.'

'You?' Sara stared at the rigid wall of his back in blank incredulity. 'But why should they want to do that? You disowned her!' she cried.

'But the world does not know that.'

Sara went cold. Stone-still, icy cold as realisation
slapped her full in the face. 'You mean—?' She
swallowed, having to battle to rise above a new kind of
fear suddenly clutching at her breast. She had banked
on this being his doing. Banked on it so much that it
came as a desperate blow to have him place an alternative
in her mind.

'I am a powerful man.' He stated the unarguable.
'Power brings its own enemies—'

But—'No.' She was shaking her head in denial even
before he'd finished speaking. 'No,' she repeated. 'This
is family stuff. I know it is. I spoke to them on the—'

'You spoke to them?' He turned, those predator's eyes
suddenly razor-like with surprise.

'On the phone.' She nodded, swallowing as the terrible sickness she had experienced during that dreadful
call came back to torment her.

'When?' His voice had roughened, hardened. He
didn't like it that she had been able to tell him something
he had not been told already. It pricked his insufferable
belief that he was omnipotent, the man who knew everything. 'When did this telephone conversation take place?'

'A-about an hour after they t-took her,' she whispered, then added bitterly, 'They said you would know
what to do!' She stared at him in despair, her summer-
blue eyes suddenly turned into dark, dark pools in an
agonised face. 'Well, do it, Nicolas!' she cried. 'For
God's sake do it!'

He muttered a violent curse, and was suddenly at her
side again, hard fingers coiling around her slender arm,
brooking no protest this time as he pushed her back into
the sofa.

'Now listen...' he said, coming to sit down beside her.
'I need to know what they said to you, Sara. And I need
to know how they said it. You understand?'

Understand? Of course she understood! 'You want to
know if they were Sicilian,' she choked. 'Well, yes! They
were Sicilian—likc you!' she said accusingly. 'I recog-

nised the accent, the same blinding contempt for any-thing and anyone who is not of the same breed!'

He ignored all of that. 'Male or female?' he persisted.

'M-male,' she breathed.

'Old—young—could you tell?'

She shook her head. 'M-muffled. The v-voice was m-muffled—by something held over the m-mouthpiece, I think.' Then she gagged, her hand whipping up to cover her quivering mouth.

Yet, ruthlessly, he reached up to catch the hand, re-moved it, held it trapped in his own in a firm command for attention.

'Did he speak in English?'

She nodded. 'But with a Sicilian accent. Let go of me...'

He ignored that. 'And what did he say? Exactly, Sara,' he insisted. 'What did he say?'

She began to shake all over—shake violently, eyes closing as she locked herself onto that terrible conver-sation that had confirmed her worst fears. '"We h-have your ch-child,"' she quoted, word for mind-numbing word. Her fingers were icy cold and trembling so badly that he began gently chafing them with his own. '"Sh-she is s-safe for now. Get S-Santino. He will know wh-what to do. We w-will contact you again at seven-th-thirty..."' Dazedly she glanced around the room. 'What time is it?' she asked jerkily.

'Shush. Not yet six,' he murmured calmingly. 'Con-centrate, Sara. Did he say anything else? Did you hear anything else? Any background sound, other voices, a plane, a car—anything?'

She shook her head. 'N-nothing.' No sound. Only the voice. Not even the sound of a child crying— 'Oh, God.' She whipped her hand out from between his to cover her eyes. 'My baby,' she whispered. 'My poor baby...I want her here!' She turned on him, holding out her arms and looking lost and tormented and heart-rendingly pa-thetic. 'In my arms...' Her arms folded and closed

around her slender body, hugging, hugging as if the small
child were already there and safe. 'Oh, God,' she
groaned. 'Oh, God, Nicolas, do something. Do
something!'

'OK,' he muttered, but distractedly. 'OK. It will be
done. But I want to know why the hell I was not informed of this telephone conversation. Was it taped?'
He was frowning blackly. 'The police have a trace on
this line. It must have been taped!'

'Afraid someone may recognise the voice?' she seared
at him scathingly. His golden eyes withered her with a
look, then he climbed grimly to his feet. Alarm shot
through her. 'Where are you going?' she bit out shrilly.

Glancing down at her, he could have been hewn from
stone again. 'To do something about this, as you requested,' he replied. 'In the meantime I suggest you go
to your room and try to rest.' His gaze flicked dispas-
sionately over her. 'I will keep you informed of any
developments.'

'Leave it all to you, you mean,' she surmised from
that.

His cool nod confirmed it. 'It is, after all, why I am
here.'

The only reason why he was here. 'Where were you?'
she asked him, curious suddenly. 'When they told you.
Where were you?'

'New York.'

She frowned. 'New York? But it's been only six hours
since—'

'Concorde,' he drawled—then added tauntingly, 'Still
suspecting me of stealing your child?'

Her chin came up, bitterness turning her blue eyes as
cold as his tiger ones. 'We both know you're quite
capable of it,' she said.

'But why should I want to?' he quite sensibly pointed
out. 'She bears no threat to me.'

'No?' Sara questioned that statement. 'Until he rids
himself of one wife and finds himself another, Lia is the

legitimate heir of Nicolas Santino. Whether or not he was man enough to conceive her.'

As a provocation it was one step too far. She knew it even as his eyes flashed, and he was suddenly leaning over her, his white teeth glinting dangerously between tightened lips, the alluring scent of his aftershave completely overlaid by the stark scent of danger. 'Take care, *wife*,' he grited, 'what you say to me!'

'And you take care,' she threw shakily back, 'that you hand my baby back to me in one whole and hearty piece. Or so help me, Nicolas,' she vowed, 'I will drag the Santino name through the gutters of every tabloid in the world!'

The eyes flashed again, black spiralling into gold as they burned into blue. 'To tell them—what?' he demanded thinly. 'What vile crime do you believe you can lay at my feet, eh? Have I not given you and your child everything you could wish for? My home,' he listed. 'My money. And, not least, my name!'

Every one of which Sara saw entirely as her due. 'And for whose sake?' she derided him scathingly. 'Your own sake, Nicolas.' She gave the answer for him. 'To protect your own Sicilian pride!'

'What pride?' Abruptly he straightened and turned away. 'You killed my pride when you took another man to your bed.'

Her heart squeezed in a moment's pained sympathy for this man who had lived with that belief for the last three years. And he was right; even if what he was saying was wrong, simply believing it to be true must have dealt a lethal blow to his monumental pride.

'Ah!' His hand flew out, long, sculptured fingers flicking her a gesture of distaste. 'I will not discuss this with you any further. You disgust me. I disgust myself even bothering to talk to you.' He turned, striding angrily to the door.

'Nicolas!' Forcing her stiff and aching limbs to propel her to her feet again, she stopped him as he went to leave the room.

He paused with his hand on the doorknob, his long body lean and lithe and pulsing with contempt. He did not turn back to face her, and tears—weak tears which came from that deep, dark well where she now kept the love she'd once felt for him—burned suddenly in her eyes.

'Nicolas—please...' she pleaded. 'Whatever you believe about me, Lia has committed no crime!'

'I know that,' he answered stiltedly.

The wretched sound of her anxiety wrenched from her in a sob. 'Then please—please get her safely back for me!'

Her plea stiffened his spine, made the muscles in the side of his neck stand out in response as he turned slightly to face her. His eyes, those hard, cold, angry eyes, fixed on the way she was standing there with her waist-length, gossamer-fine hair pushed back from her small face by a padded velvet band. She wasn't tall, and the simple style of her clothes accentuated her fine-boned slenderness.

A delicate creature. Always appearing as though the slightest puff of wind might blow her over. That a harsh word would cast her into despair. Yet—

If it was possible, the eyes hardened even more. 'The child was taken because she bears my name,' he stated coldly. 'I shall therefore do my best to return her to you unharmed.'

The door closed, leaving Sara staring angrily at the point where his stiff body had last been.

'The child', she was thinking bitterly. He referred to Lia as 'the child' as if she were a doll without a soul! A mere inanimate object which had been stolen. And because he accepted some twisted sense of responsibility for the crime he was therefore also willing to accept that it was his duty to get *it* back!

How kind! she thought as her trembling legs forced her to drop into a nearby chair. How magnanimous of him! Would he be that detached if he truly believed Lia was his own daughter? Or would he be the one requiring the reviving brandy, the one people were dying to pump sleeping pills into because they couldn't cope with the horror of it all—the horror of their baby being snatched and carried away by some ruthless, evil monster? A monster, moreover, who was prepared to stop at nothing to get what he wanted from them!

'Oh, God,' she choked, burying her face in her hands in an effort to block out her thoughts because they were so unbearable.

Her baby, in the hands of a madman. Her baby, frightened and bewildered as to what was happening to her. Her baby, wanting her mama and not understanding why she was not there when she had always been there for her before—always!

What kind of unfeeling monster would take a small child away from her mama? she wondered starkly. What made a person that bad inside? That cruel? That—?

She stopped, dragging her hands from her face as a sudden thought leapt into her head.

There really was only one person she knew who was capable of doing something like this.

Alfredo Santino. Father to the son. And ten times more ruthless than Nicolas could ever learn to be.

And he hated Sara. Hated her for daring to think herself good enough for his wonderful son. He was the man who had vowed retribution on her for luring his son away from the high-powered Sicilian marriage he'd had mapped out for him, which had then made the father look a fool in the eyes of his peers—if Alfredo Santino accepted anyone as his peer, that was. If Nicolas saw himself as omnipotent, then the father considered himself the same but more so.

But Alfredo had already exacted his retribution on her, surely? She frowned. So why—?

'No.' Suddenly she was on her feet again, still trembling—not with weakness this time but with a stark, clamouring fear that made it a struggle even to keep upright as she stumbled across the drawing-room floor and out into the hall.

CHAPTER TWO

A BIG man in a grey suit and with a tough-looking face stood guard just outside the door. A stranger. 'Where is Nicolas?' she asked shakily. 'M-my husband, where is he?'

His gaze drifted towards the closed study door. 'Mr Santino wished not to be disturbed.'

Sicilian. His accent was as Sicilian as the voice that had spoken to her on the phone. She shuddered and stepped past him, ignoring the very unsubtle hint in his reply, to hurry across the hallway and push open the study door.

He was half sitting on the edge of the big solid oak desk and he wasn't alone. The two policemen were with him, and someone she instantly recognised as Nicolas's right-hand man. Toni Valetta. All of them were in a huddle around something on the desk with their heads tilted down. But they shot upright in surprise at her abrupt entrance.

She ignored them all, her anxious eyes homing in on the only one in this room who counted. 'Nicolas . . .' She took a couple of urgent steps towards him. 'I—'

His hand snaked out—not towards her but to something on the desk. And it was only as she heard an electronic click followed by a sudden deathly silence that it hit her just what had been going on here, and what her ears had just picked up but her mind had refused to recognise until Nicolas had rendered the room silent.

God. She stopped, went white, closed her eyes, swayed. It had been her Lia's voice, her baby murmuring, 'Mama? Mama?' before it had been so severely cut off.

'Don't touch her!'

21

The command was barked from a raspingly threatening throat.

She didn't know who had tried to touch her, who had reached her first as she began to sink, as if in slow motion, to the thick carpet beneath her feet. But she recognised Nicolas's arms as they came around her, breaking her fall, catching her to his chest and holding her there as something solid hit the back of her knees, impelling her to sit down.

He didn't leave go, lowering his body with hers as he guided her into the chair, so that she could still lean weakly against him. Her heart had accelerated out of all control, her breathing fast and shallow, her mind—her mind blanked out by a horror that was more than she could bear.

And he was cursing softly, roundly, cursing in Italian, in English, cursing over her head at someone, cursing at her. Her fingers came up, ice-cold and numb, scrambling over his shirtfront and up his taut throat until they found his mouth, tight-lipped with fury.

She could have slapped him full in the face for the reaction she got. He froze, right there in front of all those watching faces; he froze into a statue of stunned silence with her trembling fingers pressed against his mouth.

'Nic,' she whispered frailly, not even knowing that she had shortened his name to that more intimate version she'd rarely used to call him, and only then when she'd been totally, utterly lost in him. 'My baby. That was my baby...'

Nicolas Santino, squatting there with her wonderful hair splayed across his big shoulders so that the sweet rose scent of it completely surrounded him, closed his hard eyes on a moment of stark, muscle-locking pain.

Then, 'Shush,' he murmured, and reached up to grasp the fingers covering his mouth, touching them briefly to his lips before clasping them gently in his hand. 'Sara, she is fine. She is asking for you but she is not distressed. You understand me, *cara*? She is—'

She passed out. At last—and perhaps it seemed fortunate to all those who had worriedly observed her all day—she finally caved in beneath the pressure of it all and went limp against the man holding her.

She came around to find herself in her own room, lying on her own bed, with the doctor leaning over her. He smiled warmly but briefly. 'I want you to take these, Mrs Santino,' he murmured, holding two small white pills and a glass of water out to her.

But she shook her head, closing her eyes again while she tried to remember what had happened. She remembered running across the hall, remembered opening the door to the study and racing inside, but what she couldn't remember was why she'd felt the dire need to go there. She remembered seeing Nicolas in the room, and Toni and the two policemen. She remembered them all jerking to attention at her rude entry and her taking several steps towards Nicolas. Then—

Oh, God. Full recall shuddered through her on a nauseous wave. 'Where's Nicolas?' she gasped.

'Here,' his grim voice replied.

Her eyes flickered open to find him looking down at her from the other side of the bed. He looked different somehow, as if some of his usual arrogance had been stripped away. 'You heard from them, didn't you?' she whispered faintly. 'They called before the deadline.' Tears pushed into her eyes. 'They let my baby talk to you.'

The corner of his tensely held mouth ticked. 'Take the two pills the doctor is offering you, Sara,' was all he said by way of a reply.

She shook her head in refusal again. 'I want to know what they said,' she insisted.

'When you take the two pills, I will tell you what they said.'

But still she refused. 'You just want to put me to sleep. And I won't be put to sleep!'

'They are not sleeping tablets, Mrs Santino,' the doctor asserted. 'You won't sleep if you don't want to, but they will help to relax you a little. I'm telling you the truth,' he tagged on gravely as her sceptical gaze drifted his way.

'I can understand your need to remain alert throughout this ordeal, but I doubt your ability to do so if you don't accept some help. Shock and stress should not be treated lightly. You're near a complete collapse,' he diagnosed. 'Another shock like the one you received downstairs may just have the effect you've been fighting so hard against and shut you down completely. Take the pills.' He offered them to her again. 'Trust me.'

Trust him. She looked into his gravely sympathetic eyes and wondered if she could trust any man in almost three years.

Not any man.

'Take the pills, Sara.' Nicolas placed his own weight behind the advice, voice grim, utterly unmoving. 'Or watch me hold you down while the doctor sticks a hypodermic syringe in your arm.'

She took the pills. Nicolas had not and never would make idle threats. And she wasn't a fool. She knew that if they did resort to a needle it would not be injecting a relaxing aid into her system.

Nobody spoke for several minutes after that, Sara lying there with her eyes closed, the doctor standing by the bed with her wrist gently clasped between his finger and thumb, and the silence was so profound that she fancied she could actually hear the light tick of someone's watch as it counted out the seconds.

She knew even before the doctor dropped her wrist and gave the back of her hand a pat that her pulse had lost that hectic flurry it had had for the last several hours and returned to a more normal rate. She sensed the two men exchanging glances then heard the soft tread of feet moving across the room. The bedroom door opened and closed, then once again she was alone with Nicolas.

'You can tell me what happened now,' she murmured, not bothering to open her eyes. 'I won't have hysterics.'

'You did not have hysterics before,' he pointed out.

'Déjà vu, Nicolas?' she taunted wanly.

To her surprise, he admitted it. 'Yes,' he said. It made her open her eyes. 'Only last time you left me there, as I remember it.'

He turned away, ostensibly simply to hunt out a chair, which he drew up beside the bed, then sat down. But really she knew that he was turning away from the memory she had just evoked—of him looking murderous, fit to actually reach out and hit her, and her responding to the threat of it by passing out.

Only that particular incident had taken place in another house, another country, in another world altogether. And that time he had walked out and left her lying there.

She had not set eyes on him again until today.

'When did they call?' she asked.

'Just after I left you.'

'What did they say?'

That well-defined shadow called a mouth flexed slightly. 'You really don't need to know what they said,' he advised her. 'Let us just leave it that they wished me to be aware that they mean business.'

'What kind of business?' It was amazing, Sara noted as an absent aside, how two small pills could take all the emotion out of her. 'Money business?'

His mouth took on a cynical tilt. 'I would have thought it obvious that they want money, since it is the one commodity I have in abundance.'

She nodded in agreement, then totally threw him by saying flatly, 'It's a lie. They don't want your money.'

He frowned. 'And how do you come to that conclusion?'

'Because they are Sicilian,' she said, as if that made everything clear. But just in case it didn't she spelled it out for him. 'If you'd said they'd taken her as part of a vendetta because you'd spoiled some big business deal of theirs or something I might have believed you. But not simply for money.'

'Are you by any chance still suspecting me of this crime?' he enquired very coolly.

If she could have done, Sara would have smiled at his affronted manner. But, having gone from rigid-tight to liquid-slack, her muscles were allowing her to do nothing other than lie here heavily on this bed.

'Not you,' she said flatly, 'but your father.'

That hardened him, honed away every bit of softening she'd seen in his face as he struck her with a narrowed glare. 'Leave my father out of this,' he commanded grimly.

'I wish I could,' she said. 'But I can't. You crossed him when you married me,' she reminded him. 'He never forgave me for that. And you're still crossing him now, by refusing to finish our marriage and find yourself another wife. How long do you think a man of his calibre will let such a situation go on before he decides to do something about it himself?'

'By stealing your child?' His derision was spiked. 'How, with your logic, does that make me jump to my father's bidding?'

Her eyes, bruised and darkened by anxiety, suddenly flickered into a clear and cynical brilliance. 'It has brought you here, hasn't it?' she pointed out. 'Made you face a mistake you have been refusing to face for three whole years.'

To her surprise, he laughed—not nicely but scathingly. 'If those are my father's tactics then he has made a grave error of judgement. What's mine I keep,' His eyes narrowed coldly on her. 'And though I will never wish to lay a finger on you myself again in this lifetime I am equally determined that no other man will have the privilege.'

The words sent a chill through her. 'Your own personal vendetta, Nicolas?' she taunted softly.

'If you like,' He didn't deny it.

Sara lifted a limp hand to cover her aching eyes. 'Then perhaps you should inform your father of that,' she said wearily.

'I don't need to,' he drawled. 'He already knows it. And even if he does pine for the day his son rids himself of one wife to get himself another,' he went on grimly, 'he is in no fit state to do anything about it.'

He got up, shifting the chair back to where he'd got it from, then turned back towards her, his face suddenly carved from stone again. 'You see, six months ago my father suffered a heart attack.' He watched coldly the way her hand slid away from her shocked eyes. 'It has left him weak in health and wheelchair-bound, barely fit to function unaided, never mind plot anything as underhand as this.'

Suddenly he was leaning over her again, intimidating and serious with it. 'So keep your nasty insinuations about my father to yourself, Sara,' he warned her. 'It is one thing you daring to insult me with your twisted view of my family, but my father is off limits; do you understand?'

'Yes,' she whispered, stunned—stunned to her very depths at the piece of news he had given her. Alfredo sick? she was thinking dazedly. That big, bullying man confined to a wheelchair? I'm sorry,' she said, meaning it—not for Alfredo but for Nicolas, who worshipped his father.

'I do not need your sympathy,' he said as he straightened. 'Just a curb on your vile tongue where he is concerned.'

A knock at the door heralded Toni's urgent appearance in the doorway. He glanced warily at Sara then at his employer. 'They're on the phone again.'

Nicolas moved—so did Sara, lurching off the bed with a mixture of stark urgency and dizzying exhaustion to land swaying on her feet.

'No,' Nicolas said. 'You stay here.' He was already striding towards the door.

Her blue eyes lifted in horror. 'Nic—please!' She went to stumble after him.

'No,' he repeated brutally. 'Make her,' he instructed Toni as he went by him.

The door closed. 'I hate him,' she whispered in angry frustration. 'I hate him!'

'He is merely thinking of you, Sara,' Toni Valetta put in gently. 'It would not be pleasant being witness to the kind of discussion he is about to embark on.'

She laughed, much as Nicolas had laughed minutes ago—bitterly, scathingly. 'You mean the one where he barters for my daughter's life?'

Toni studied her wretched face but said nothing; she was only stating the raw truth of it, after all.

'Oh, damn it,' she whispered, and wilted weakly back onto the edge of the bed. Whether it was the acceptance of that truth or the pills the doctor had administered that took the legs from her she didn't know, but suddenly she found she did not have the necessary strength to remain standing any longer.

There was an uncomfortable silence, in which the man remained hovering by the closed bedroom door and Sara sat slumped, fighting the waves of exhaustion flooding through her.

'Go away, Toni,' she muttered eventually. 'Don't worry. I won't get you in trouble with your boss by making a bolt for the study as soon as your back is turned.'

His sigh was almost sad, but he did not leave; instead he moved over to stand by the window. 'I may not be the perfect choice of companion just now,' he replied heavily, 'but we used to be friends, Sara.'

Friends, she repeated to herself. Was that what they once had been? She knew Toni Valetta from years ago. He was Nicolas's tall, dark, handsome assistant. Together they made an invincible team—Toni the smooth, smiling charmer, Nicolas the ice-cold operator. Anything Nicolas could not do himself he entrusted to Toni, and Toni's loyalty to Nicolas was unimpeachable; the two men's relationship was that close. Once, years ago, Sara had believed his loyalty to Nicolas had broadened to encompass her as well. And she had considered him her friend—her only friend in a world of enemies. She had felt so alone then, so cut off from reality, bewildered by the new, rich, high-society life that

Nicolas had propelled her into, and afraid of those people who openly resented her presence in it.

Toni had been the only person she could turn to in times of need when Nicolas was not there.

But when the chips had been stacked against her even Toni had turned his back on her.

'I need no one,' she said now, making her backbone erect. 'Only my baby.'

He nodded once, slowly, his gaze fixed on the garden outside. 'Nic will get her back for you,' he said with a quiet confidence that actually managed to soothe a little of that gnawing ache she was living with inside. He turned then, his dark brown eyes levelling sombrely on her. 'But you have to trust him to do it his way, Sara.'

Trust. She grimaced. There was that word again. Trust. 'They rang,' she said jerkily. 'Before their specified time. Did they say why they'd done that?'

He shrugged, his broad shoulders encased, like Nicolas's, in expensive dark silk. 'They were having us followed,' he explained. 'Nic and I. They tracked our journey from New York to here. I think they must have miscalculated how long it would take us to get to England and decided we couldn't make it before the time they offered you.' His grimace was almost a smile. 'It must not have occurred to them that Nic would fly Concorde...'

As he was a man who flew everywhere in his private jet, Sara could understand it. It must have been quite a culture shock for Nicolas Santino to use public transport—even if it was the best public transport in the world, she mused acidly.

'The news affected him badly, Sara,' Toni put in deeply. 'I don't think I have ever seen him so upset. Not since...'

The words tailed off. Sara didn't blame him. He had been about to say since Nic discovered her betrayal. Not quite the most diplomatic thing to have brought up right now.

'Nicolas said his father had been—ill.' Grimly she changed the subject, not wanting to hear how Nicolas had felt. She wouldn't believe Toni's interpretation of Nicolas's feelings anyway.

'A terrible business,' Toni confirmed. 'It was fortunate he was in London and not at home in Taormina when it happened, or he would not be alive today.'

London? She frowned. Alfredo had been in London six months ago when he'd been taken ill? But he never came to London. Had always professed to hate the place!

'He spent two months in hospital here before he was well enough to travel home. Nic hardly left his bedside for two weeks.'

Nicolas had been that close to this house for two weeks and she hadn't known it. She shivered.

'It was all kept very quiet, of course,' Toni continued. 'Alfredo had too many delicate fingers in too many delicate pies for it to be—safe for the news of his illness to get out. Since then, Nic has been working himself into the ground, doing the job of two.'

'Poor Nic,' she murmured without an ounce of sympathy, adding drily, 'Now this.'

Toni's eyes flashed at that—just as Nicolas's would flash to warn of the sparking of his Sicilian temper. 'Don't mock him, Sara,' he said stiffly. 'You of all people have no right to mock him! He is here, is he not?' His beautiful English began to deteriorate at the expense of his anger. 'He come to your aid without a second thought about it when most other men would have turned their back and walked the other way!'

'As you would have done?' His anger didn't subdue her. Once upon a time it might have done, but not any more. None of these people would intimidate her with their hot Sicilian temperaments and cold Sicilian pride ever again. 'Then it's no wonder Nicolas is who he is and you are only his sidekick,' she derided. 'For at least he sees people as human beings and not pawns to be used or turned away from depending on how important they are to you!'

The door flew open. Sara leapt to her feet, Toni forgotten, as Nicolas came back into the room. He paused, shooting both of them a sharp glance. The air had to be thick with their exchange. And, even if it wasn't, the way Toni was standing there, all stiff Sicilian offence, would have given the game away.

'Well?' she said anxiously. 'Have they. . .?'

The words dwindled away, his expression enough to wipe what bit of life her hot exchange with Toni had put into her face right away again.

'Be calm,' he soothed as her arms whipped around her body and she began to shiver. 'They are still negotiating. Try to keep in the front of your mind, Sara, that they want what I have the power to give them more than they want to keep your child.'

But she hardly heard him. 'Negotiating?' she choked. 'What is there to negotiate about? Pay them, Nicolas!' she cried. 'You've got money to burn! So give it to them and get my baby back!'

He grimaced—she supposed at her naïvety. But seeing it gave her pause. 'How much?' she whispered threadily.

'That part is not up for discussion,' he dismissed.

Her eyes flickered to Toni's studiedly blank face then back to Nicolas. And a low throb took up residence in her chest. 'They're asking for too much, aren't they?' she breathed. 'They want more than you can lay your hands on at such short notice.'

He smiled, not with amusement but with a kind of wry self-mockery. 'At least you are not accusing me of being tight,' he drawled.

'No.' She wasn't quite the fluffy-headed fool she sometimes sounded. She knew that people with riches made their money work for them rather than just let it take up room in some bank vault. 'So, what happens now?' she asked tensely.

'We wait.' He turned a brief nod on Toni, which was an instruction for him to leave them. The other man did as he was told, walking out of the room without saying a word.

Wait. It was over seven hours since Lia had been taken, the longest Sara had ever been without her, and it hurt—hurt so badly she could hardly bear it.

'Then what?'

'We hope by the time they call back again they will have begun to see sense.' He put it to her bluntly, as, she supposed, there was no other way to put it. 'When did you last have something to eat?'

'Hmm?' Her bruised eyes were lost in confusion, the question meaning absolutely nothing to her.

'Food,' he prompted. 'When did you last eat?'

She shook her head, lifting a hand to slide the black velvet band from her hair so that she could run shaky fingers through the thick silken strands. 'I can't eat.'

'When?' he repeated stubbornly.

'Breakfast.' Tossing the band onto the bed, she returned to hugging herself—remembering, seeing herself as she had been that morning, happy, smiling at Lia as they'd shared breakfast, the little girl smiling back. 'Oh, God.' She folded up like a paper doll onto the edge of the bed, tears of agonised helplessness filling her eyes. 'What is it?' Nicolas said tensely.

'They won't know—will they?' she choked. 'What she likes to eat or how she likes to eat it. She'll be confused and start fretting. And she'll wonder why I'm not there with her. She—'

'Stop it.' Grimly he came to squat down in front of her. 'Listen to me, Sara. You cannot allow your mind to drift like that. Children are by nature resilient creatures. She will cope—probably better than you are coping. But you must help yourself by trying not to torment yourself like this or you will not stay the course.'

He was right. She knew it, and made a mammoth effort to calm herself, nodding her agreement, blinking away the tears. 'Did—?' Carefully she moistened paper-dry lips. 'Did they let you hear her again?'

His eyes, usually so coldly tigerish, were darker than usual. Almost as if against his wishes, his hand came up to brush her long hair away from her pale cheek.

'She is fine,' he murmured. 'I could hear her in the background chatting happily.'

'Did you record it?' she asked eagerly. 'I want to hear it.'

'No.' Suddenly he was on his feet, the cold, remote stranger he had arrived here as.

'But why not?' she demanded bewilderedly. 'I need to hear her—can't you understand that?'

'I can understand it,' he conceded. 'But I will not give in to it. It will distress you too much, so don't bother asking again.'

Stiffly he moved back towards the door, the discussion obviously over. Then he stopped, his attention caught by something standing on the polished walnut bureau. Sara's gaze followed his—then went still, just as everything inside her went still, even her breathing, as slowly he reached out with a long-fingered hand and picked up the framed photograph.

'She is very like you,' he observed after a long, taut moment.

'Yes,' was all she could manage in reply, because the facts were all there in that picture. Golden hair, pure blue eyes, pale, delicate skin. Lia was Sara's double. She bore no resemblance whatsoever to her father.

'She is very beautiful,' he added gruffly. 'You must love her very much.'

'Oh, Nicolas,' she cried, her chest growing heavy—heavy with despair for both man and child who had been robbed of their right to know and love each other. 'As you should love her! She's—!'

Your daughter too! she had been about to say. But he stopped her. 'No!' he cut in harshly—making Sara wince as he rejected both her claim and Lia's picture by snapping it back onto the polished top. 'You will not begin spouting those—frankly insulting claims all over again.' He turned, his face as coldly closed as she had ever seen it, golden eyes slaying her as they flicked over her in a contemptuous act of dismissal. 'I am not here to listen to your lies. I am here to recover your child.

Your child!' he emphasised bitterly. 'Whoever the father is, it certainly is not me!'

'Yours,' she repeated, defiant in the face of his contempt. 'Your child, your conception—your betrayal of a trust I had a right to expect from you! Do you think it isn't equally insulting for me to know you can suspect me of being unfaithful to you? When?' she demanded. 'When did I ever give you reason to believe I could be capable of such a despicable crime? Me?' she choked, 'Go with another man? I was shy! So shy I would blush and stammer like an idiot if one so much as spoke to me!'

'Until you learned to taste your own powers over my sex,' he asserted. 'The powers I taught you to recognise!' He gave a deriding flick of his hand. 'Then you no longer blushed or stammered. You smiled and flirted!'

'I never did!' she denied hotly. 'My shyness irritated you so I strove to suppress it. But I would have had to have undergone a complete personality change to manage to flirt with anyone!'

'Not while I was there, no,' he agreed.

'And not while you were away!' she insisted. 'I tried to be what I thought you wanted me to be!' She appealed to his intelligence for understanding. 'I tried to behave as the other women behaved. I tried to become the upstanding member of your social circle you kept on telling me I should be! I tried very hard for your sake!'

'Too hard, then,' he clipped out. 'For I do not recall encouraging you to take a lover for my sake.'

'I did not take a lover,' she sighed.

'So the man I saw you wrapped in the arms of was a figment of my imagination, was he?' he taunted jeeringly.

'No,' she conceded, her arms wrapping around her own body in shuddering memory of that scene. 'He was real.'

'And in five weeks I had not so much as touched you, yet you still managed to become pregnant—a miracle,' he added.

'Your mathematics are poor,' she said. 'It was four weeks. And we made love several times that night.'

'And the next day you got your period which therefore cancels out that night.'

Sara sighed at that one, heavily, defeatedly. She had lied to him that next day. Lied because he had just told her that he was going away and she'd wanted to punish him for leaving her again so soon. She had concocted the lie which would deprive him of her body—and had learned to regret the lie every single day of her life since.

All of which she had confessed to him before without it making an ounce of difference to what he believed, so she was not going to try repeating it again now.

'No ready reply to that one, I note,' he drawled when she offered nothing in return.

Sara shook her head. 'Believe what you want to believe,' she tossed at him wearily. 'It really makes little difference to me any more...' She meant it, too; her expression told him so as she lifted blue eyes dulled of any hint of life to his. 'I once loved you more than life itself. Now my love for Lia takes precedence over anything I ever felt for you.'

All emotion was honed out of his face at that. 'Tidy yourself,' he instructed, turning with cold dismissal back to the door. 'Then come downstairs. I will go and arrange for something to eat.'

CHAPTER THREE

THE house had returned to its usual smooth running. Mrs Hobbit, the housekeeper, bustled about. Mr Hobbit, Sara noticed when she glanced out of her bedroom window before going down, was busily working on the new play area he and Sara had been planning at the bottom of the garden. It wrenched at her heart to see him rhythmically spreading bark chippings over the specially prepared patch where, next week, a garden swing and slide were due to be fixed—yet, oddly, it comforted her. Mr Hobbit had not given up hope of Lia's return and neither would she.

When she eventually made herself go downstairs to the dining room she found Nicolas standing at the window watching the old man at his work. It was June and the sun set late in the evenings. You could work outside until ten o'clock if you were so inclined. This evening the garden was bathed in a rich coral glow that cast a warmth over everything, including Nicolas.

Something stirred inside her—something long, long suppressed. The ache of a woman for the man she loved.

And for a moment she couldn't move or speak, couldn't let him know she was there because she was suddenly seeing another man from another time who used to stand by the window like that. A man whom she would have gone to join, slipping her arm through the crook of his and leaning against him while she described all the plans she had made for their garden. Their daughter.

How would Nicolas have responded if things had not been as they were between them and she had been able to go freely and tell him what Mr Hobbit was doing? Would he have been amused? Interested? Would he have

36

wanted to join in the planning of their child's first play garden?

Her eyes glazed over, sudden tears blurring his silhouette as rain would against a sheet of glass.

The first time she had met Nicolas it had been raining, Sara recalled. Not the fine summer rain you tended to get at this time of year, but a sudden heavy cloudburst that had sent people running in an effort to get out of it as soon as they could.

She'd been a very ordinary assistant in a big garden centre on the outskirts of central London then. Twenty-one years old and so painfully shy that her cheeks flushed if a stranger so much as smiled at her, she had been more happy to spend her time amongst the shrubs and plants than to deal with customers. But the garden centre had run a plant service whereby they'd provided and cared for the plants the big office blocks in the city liked to decorate their foyers with. One aspect of her job had been to attend to a certain section of these 'rentals', as they called them. But it had taken every ounce of courage she possessed to walk into some of the palatial foyers on her list.

The shyness had been left over from the quiet, lonely childhood spent with her widowed, ageing father who had taken early retirement from teaching when his wife had died leaving him solely responsible for their only child. They'd moved away from the quiet London suburb to the wild, lonely fells of Yorkshire, where he'd decided to teach his daughter himself rather than send her the five miles to the nearest school.

She was thirteen years old when he died, quite suddenly, of a heart attack while walking on his beloved fells. The first thing Sara knew of it was when his dog, Sammie, came back without him, whimpering at the cottage door.

After that she was sent to a boarding-school to finish her education, paid for out of her father's estate. But by then the shyness was already an inherent part of her and she found it difficult if not painful to interact with any of the other girls. She coped, though—barely, but she coped—learned to deal with other people on a quiet, timid level. But she did not manage to make any real friends, and spent most of her free time wandering around the school's private grounds, which was probably how she developed such an interest in plants—that and the fact that the school's resident gardener was a quiet little man who reminded her of her father, which meant she could at least relax with him.

It was with his quiet encouragement that she discovered she had a flair for gardening. Green-fingered, he called it—an ability to make anything grow—and she would have gone on to horticultural college after leaving the school, but then another disaster struck when she contracted glandular fever just before her final exams, which stopped her taking them. The virus lingered with her for over a year. By the time it had gone, so had her funds. And rather than take her exams a year late then try for college she had to get herself a job instead.

Which was why she was in that particular street in London the day she bumped into Nicolas—literally bumped into him, she on her way back from attending to her customer list, he as he climbed out of a black cab.

It was lunchtime. A heavy downpour of rain had just opened up. People were running, as was Sara herself—hurrying, with her head down as a black cab drew up at the kerb just in front of her. The door flew open and a man got out, almost knocking her off her feet when they collided.

'Apologies,' he clipped. That was all; she didn't think he even glanced at her then, just strode off across the flow of rushing pedestrians and into the nearest building.

That should have been the end of it. And sometimes when she looked back she found herself wishing that it had been the end of it. Her life would have been so different if Nicolas had not come barging into it as he had. But then at other times she could only count her blessings, because without knowing him she would not have learned that she could love another person as deeply as she had learned to love him—she had been too shy to experiment with feelings at all, until she'd met him. She would not have learned about her own simmering passions or how they could overpower any shyness when coaxed to do so by a man whose own passions ran hot and dynamic through his blood.

And she would not have known the greatest loves of all. The love of a child for its mother. And the love a mother could feel for her child.

So no, no matter what had happened to them since, she was not sorry now that her first encounter with Nicolas had not been the last encounter. But coming into contact with a man of Nicolas Santino's dynamic personality had been a bit like being a dove devoured by an eagle.

He'd dropped his wallet. Right at her feet and in the pouring rain. He had stalked off without knowing he had dropped it, having absently tried to shove the wallet back into his jacket pocket.

Standing there with the rain pouring down on her head and still feeling a bit winded by the way he had bumped into her, she had taken a moment to realise what it was that had fallen onto her feet. She'd bent, picked it up, glanced a bit dazedly around her for a sign of what to do next. He had already disappeared into the building by then, and logic had told her that she really had no choice but to follow him.

The rest, she supposed, was history—her following him into the building, luckily seeing him standing by the reception desk with a bevy of dark-suited men around him all shaking hands, her approaching shyly.

'Excuse me...' Tentatively she touched his arm.

He turned, looked down at her, and she could still remember the way his golden eyes made her quiver oddly inside as they lanced into her.

The soft green sweatshirt she was wearing, with the logo of the garden centre she worked for emblazoned on the front, was wet through. Her hair, braided in a single thick plait, dripped water down her back. Her face was wet, not to mention her jean-clad legs and trainers. He took it all in seemingly without needing to remove his gaze from her blushing face.

'Yes?' he prompted.

'I th-think you dropped th-this when you bumped into me just n-now . . .' Nervously she held out the wallet towards him. 'Could y-you please check if it's y-yours?'

It was sheer reaction that sent his hands up to pat his pockets. But he did not take his eyes off her face. A small silence developed while she held out the wallet and he ignored it. A couple of the entourage gathered around him shuffled their feet when they picked up on the sudden tension flowing through the air.

He was tall and she wasn't, the top of her head barely reaching his chin, so she had to tilt her head to look into his face. The rain had caught him too, but only briefly, so the drops sat on the expensive silk of his jacket in small crystal globules that could easily be brushed away. His hair was so black that it reminded her of midnight, gleaming damply but not dripping wet like hers.

She didn't know then that the great Nicolas Santino stood there like that in silence because he was completely and utterly love-struck. He admitted that to her later—weeks later when his single-minded campaign to break through her shy reserve was successful—on a night when she lay in his arms on a bed of fine linen, their bodies damp, limbs tangled, his hand gently stroking her long hair across the pillow. And she was shy—still shy even though he had just guided her through the most intimate journey a man and woman could share with each other.

A week after that, they married in a registry office in London. That was the first time she met Toni—when he stood witness for Nicolas. She remembered how strangely he looked at her—as if he couldn't believe the kind of woman his employer had decided to marry. And the hushed conversation they'd shared before they'd gone in to the ceremony had confirmed his disbelief.

'What the hell are you playing at, Nic?' he'd muttered urgently. 'She doesn't look strong enough to manage you, never mind a hostile father-in-law!'

Hostile? She had begun to get very nervous at that point, frightened even. But then Nicolas had smiled. She could still conjure up that smile now and feel the warmth of it fill her.

'She manages me fine,' he had murmured softly. 'She is my opposite in every way that matters and with her I am complete. She will manage my father as well; you will see,' he'd ordained.

He had been wrong. She had not managed his father. In fact, she had been terrified of him from their first meeting. He was a sly, selfish, power-hungry and nasty old man who'd seen her as the single obstacle spoiling the glorious plans he had made for his only child. But he was also clever—clever enough never to let Nicolas see how much he hated Sara for getting in the way of those plans.

Oh, he voiced his initial disappointment in his son's choice of bride, showed anger, a bitter scepticism of the English in general and of Sara's ability to cope with the kind of lifestyle they led. Then when he met the brick wall of his son's own determination to run his life his own way he stepped back to the sidelines and watched and plotted and waited for his moment to pounce.

He picked up on her shyness and timidity straight away and used it ruthlessly against her, forcing her into situations where she would feel totally out of her depth. He knew the great Santino wealth and power intimidated her. He knew she only felt comfortable when Nicolas was at her side, so he arranged it so that Nicolas was hardly ever there.

And Alfredo put himself up as her escort, cloaking his hostility towards her in the presence of his son, displaying a willingness to be Sara's mentor while she got used to the kind of socialising expected of a Santino woman—while Nicolas got on with more important things, like running the Santino empire.

Consequently, she spent the first year of her marriage in a bewildering world of fine clothes and expensive cars and brittle, bright, sophisticated people who were quite happy to follow the great Alfredo Santino's lead and mock his very unsophisticated daughter-in-law whenever the chance arose. The fact that on the few occasions she tried to tell Nicolas this he got angry and actually took offence on his father's behalf only made her feel more helplessly out of her depth, more isolated, more miserable.

It began to put a strain on their marriage. When Nicholas was home, his father would be all charm, which made Sara tense up with a wariness her husband could not understand. When they went out together, the same people who followed Alfredo's lead would now follow Nicolas's lead and treat his wife with a warmth she was, quite naturally, suspicious of and Nicolas saw as her being standoffish and cold.

Then a man—an Englishman, Jason Castell—began showing her a lot of attention. Whenever she was out with Alfredo, he would appear at her side, sit with her, dance with her, forever trying to monopolise her attention. If she was out with Nicolas, Jason would be conspicuous in his absence.

Yet Nicolas still heard about him. 'Who is this Englishman I hear you've befriended?' he asked her one evening as they were getting ready for bed.

'Who, Jason?' she asked. 'He's a friend of your father's, not mine.'

'That is not how I hear it,' he said coolly. 'I would prefer it if my wife did not have her name connected with another man. Break the friendship, Sara,' he warned. 'Or watch me break it for you.'

For some time her desire to fight back, if only with Nicolas, had been growing stronger the more pressure Alfredo applied to her nerves. And this once she retaliated, hard and tight. 'If you can rarely be bothered to be here with me yourself, then I don't see what right you have to tell me who I can and cannot spend my time with.'

'I have the right of a husband,' he arrogantly replied.

'Is that what you call yourself? I call you the man who occasionally visits my bed! How long have you been away this time, Nicolas?' she demanded as his eyes flashed a warning. 'Two, nearly three weeks? What am I supposed to do with myself when you're not here—hide away in purdah?' In her mind this was not an argument about Jason Castell, but about their lifestyle in general. 'If you want to know what I'm doing every single minute of the day then stay around and find out!'

'I have a business to run!' he threw back harshly. 'The same business which pays for all your fine clothes and the luxury surroundings for you to wear them in!'

'And did I ask for the clothes?' she challenged. 'Did I ask for the luxury accommodation? When I fell in love with you I fell in love with the man, not his money! But I rarely see the man, do I?'

'You're seeing him now,' he murmured huskily.

And she was, seeing him in all his golden-skinned, sensually sinewed, naked glory.

But for the first time ever she turned away from the invitation his husky words had offered. 'We've been married for almost a year,' she said. 'And I can count on the fingers of one hand how many weeks we've actually spent together. This isn't even my home, it's your father's!' she sighed. 'And on the rare occasions you do find time to come here your father takes priority.'

'I refuse to pander to your unnatural jealousy of my relationship with my father,' he clipped.

'And I hate living here,' she told him bluntly. 'And if you can't be here more than you are then I want to go home, to London. I want to get a job and work to fill my days. I want a life, Nicolas,' she appealed to his steadily closing face, 'that doesn't revolve around couture shops and beauty parlours and feeling the outsider with all these tight-knit, clannish Sicilians!'

'A life with an Englishman, perhaps.'

She sighed again, irritably this time. 'This has nothing to do with Jason.'

'No?'

'No!' she denied. 'It is to do with you and me and a marriage that isn't a marriage because you aren't here enough! It's to do with me being unhappy here!' Tears, honest tears, filled her eyes at that point; she could see him blur out of focus as she appealed to him to understand. 'I can't go on like this—can't you see? They—your father, your friends—overwhelm me! I'm frightened when you're not here!'

An appeal from the heart. It should have cut into him, reminded him of the soft, gentle creature he had originally fallen in love with. The one who had been so timid that she used to cling to him when he'd introduced her to someone he knew, or had reached for his hand if they'd crossed the road, or could be tongue-tied by a painful shyness when teased.

But he was Sicilian. And a Sicilian man was by nature territorial and possessive. And if Sara dismissed Jason Castell from her mind as unimportant Nicolas didn't. Because she hadn't voiced all of these complaints before the Englishman's name had begun cropping up in conversations around the island. She hadn't dared to argue with him like this before the man had come on the scene.

And she had never turned away from the blatant invitation of his body before the Englishman's appearance.

'Get into bed,' he gritted.

'No.' She began to quiver at the expression on his face.

'I w-want to talk this through . . .'

He began striding around the bed towards her. She backed away, her hands outstretched to ward him off, long, delicately boned fingers trembling. 'Please don't,' she whispered unsteadily. 'You're frightening me. I don't want to be frightened of you too . . .'

But he wasn't listening, or maybe didn't care at that moment that he was about to murder the one firm bit of faith she had—that he, this hard-headed, ruthless hunter she had married, would not, could not hurt her.

He hurt her. Oh, not in the physical sense, but with a hard, ruthless sensuality that left her feeling ravaged to the point of shock. 'Go near the Englishman and I shall kill you both,' he then vowed tautly. 'What's mine I keep, and you are most definitely mine!'

'What's mine I keep...'

He never retracted that vow. Not throughout the following month when she never saw him, never heard from him, never left the villa. She didn't even hear Alfredo's mocking little jibes about her failing marriage and his son's preference for being anywhere but with his pathetic little wife.

She didn't so much as suspect the neat little trap that Alfredo was setting for her when he delivered a message from Nicolas one evening telling her to meet him in Catania in a hotel they had sometimes stayed in when attending some function in the city.

She arrived at the appointed suite, nervous, a little frightened, praying that he had asked her to come here because he was at last beginning to accept that she was unhappy and they needed to be alone to talk without fear of interruption. She let herself in with the provided key, took the overnight bag Nicolas had told her to bring with her through to the bedroom, then went back into the sitting room to wait.

He didn't come. By ten o'clock she was feeling let down and angry. By eleven she'd grimly got ready for bed. By twelve she was trying hard to fall asleep when she heard another key in the door. Elation sent her scrambling in her lovely cream silk nightdress out of the bed and towards the bedroom door just as it opened inwards.

Then came the shock, the horror, the confusion, because it wasn't Nicolas who came through the door but Jason. Jason, who paused in the open doorway, smiled, and murmured, 'Sara, darling, you look exquisite—as always.'

Blank incomprehension held her stunned and silent. He stepped closer, pulling her into his arms and she let him do it, utterly incapable of working out how to deal with the situation.

A mistake, she was thinking stupidly. Jason had somehow made a terrible, terrible mistake!

A hand landing hard against its wood sent the door flying open. And then Nicolas stood there. Nicolas, with his face turned to rock. Nicolas, who stared at her with his hunter's gold eyes turned yellow with shock while she stared helplessly back, the frissons of confusion, alarm, horror and shock wild inside her.

'So my father was right. You bitch,' he said. That was all.

Guilty as charged. Her silence damned her. Her blushing cheeks damned her. The way Jason made a lurching dive for the balcony doors and disappeared through them to go she neither knew nor cared where damned her. And the sheer silk nightdress bought especially for this meeting and which showed every contour of her slender body beneath damned her.

He still didn't move and neither could she. Her mind was rocketing through all the reasons why Jason could have come here believing that she was waiting for him. Then it hit her, and she went white—not with shame but with fury.

Alfredo. Alfredo had set her up—set this up! Alfredo.

'Nic—please!' Her blue eyes were slightly wild and begging. 'This isn't what you—'

He took a step towards her, his face turning from rock to murderous threat. His hand came up, the back of it aimed to lash out at her.

'No!' she cried, instinctively cowering away, long hair flying in a wild arc as her arms came up to protect her face.

It stopped him; seeing her cower like that did manage to stop him. 'For God's sake!' she pleaded, wretchedly from behind her protecting hands. 'You must listen to me!'

'Never,' he said through gritted teeth. 'You no longer exist.'

He meant it. She could see in the glacial gold of his eyes that he meant it. It was too much. She fainted at his feet. When she came round she was alone, lying where he had left her.

She hadn't so much as spoken to him again until today. She had not been allowed back in the villa. And that same hotel suite had become her prison for the next few terrible days until Toni, cold-eyed and uncommunicative, had come to personally escort her off the island and back to London.

Wretched with despair and weak with nervous reaction, she'd done as she was told, come here to this house, sat here in this house for weeks—weeks waiting for him to calm down, see sense, realise that she, of all people, could never do such a wicked thing as to take another lover.

Then she'd discovered she was pregnant, and everything had changed. She'd tried phoning him; he'd refused to take her calls. She'd tried writing to him; he hadn't acknowledged her letters. In the end she'd turned to Toni for help, called him on the phone and begged him—begged him to persuade Nicolas to see her, listen to what she had to say! 'I'm going to have his baby, Toni!' Even now, three years on, she could still hear the anguish in her voice. 'Surely that must mean something to him!'

It hadn't. The next day the phone had rung. It was Toni.

'He says you lie,' he informed her coldly. 'The child you carry cannot be his. You may have the use of the house you are in at present.' He went on in that same icy vein. 'Everything you and the child may need will be provided so long as you remain there and say nothing of your betrayal.'

'If he feels like that, then why doesn't he just throw me out on the street and divorce me?' she sliced back bitterly, hurt and angered by the injustice of it all.

'You have humiliated him enough without the added scandal of a divorce,' he clipped. 'But hear this,' he then warned icily. 'Let another man near you and he will kill you both; make no mistake about that.'

Did that mean Jason already lay dead somewhere in Sicily? she wondered, and found she couldn't care less. Jason had to have been in cahoots with Alfredo. It had not taken her long to work that one out. And for that he deserved anything Nicolas might have decided to deal out to him. It was only a shame that Alfredo would not be getting his due for his part in it all.

But maybe Alfredo had got what was due to him, she now thought as she slowly returned to the present. Because in his determination to get rid of the woman he saw as an unfit wife for his son he had lost the right to love one of the most wonderful creatures ever placed on this earth: Lia. Was he ever curious? she wondered. Did he ever just sit and wonder about his son's child who was also his grandchild? Did he ever suffer from pangs of regret?

She hoped he did. She really hoped that, sick man or not now, he suffered daily from bitter, bitter regrets.

And that, she acknowledged grimly, was her own desire for vengeance rearing its ugly head.

A movement just behind her in the doorway made her turn to find herself captured by Toni's narrowed, watchful eyes. And for a moment—a brief but stinging moment—she had a feeling he knew exactly what she had been thinking.

Then the connection was broken because Nicolas heard them and turned around. But all through dinner she felt Toni's eyes on her, and stung with the uncomfortable feeling that he had sensed her thirst for revenge.

He was Sicilian. And Sicilians claimed exclusive rights on vendettas. He would not take kindly to the idea of a mere English woman encroaching on those rights. Especially against a fellow Sicilian.

The meal was an ordeal. Sara forced down a couple of small bites of the braised chicken placed in front of her but other than that could swallow nothing. Nicolas and Toni ate with her, their occasional bursts of conversation to do with some business deal they were presently involved in. But these exchanges were brief, and largely they respected her desire to keep silent.

'Excuse me.' At last she stood up from the table, bringing both dark heads up sharply. 'I've had enough. I think I'll go and take a shower...'

'Try to rest,' Nicolas quietly advised. 'I promise I will come and tell you the moment I have any news.'

She nodded, wearied—too weary to want to argue. She wouldn't rest—she knew she wouldn't—but it was easier to let him think that she might than to battle.

She didn't think she would sleep again until she had her baby back in her arms.

CHAPTER FOUR

IT WAS a long night. Sara dozed fitfully and came down to breakfast the next morning hollow-eyed and wan-faced, to find Nicolas sitting alone at the breakfast table, a newspaper spread out in front of him.

He folded it away when he saw her, though, making a narrow-eyed study of the obvious evidence of strain in her face.

She gave an inward grimace, entirely aware of exactly how terrible she looked.

She was wearing no make-up, and the peaches-and-cream bloom that her skin usually wore was missing. She had brushed her hair, but only so she could tie it at the back to keep the long, heavy mass out of the way. And she was wearing a simple, sprigged muslin skirt teamed with a long, loose silk knit jumper in a delicate shade of blue. Under normal circumstances the pastel colour would have suited her, but today it just enhanced the washed-out look—not that she cared. She didn't care about anything to do with herself right now.

He didn't look too hot either, she noted. His lean face had a drawn quality about it that suggested he hadn't slept much himself last night. But at least the slick silk business suit had gone, his casual beige linen trousers and long-sleeved polo shirt in mint-green softening the harder edges of his tycoon persona. And the shirt was big enough not to mold his impressive torso but soft enough to make her aware of the muscled breast flexing beneath it as he moved.

'What has happened to the nanny?' she asked, pulling out a chair and sitting down. 'I went to see how she was this morning, but she wasn't there, and her room has been cleared out.'

'She was taken home to her parents last night,' he informed her. 'She was too distressed to be any use here so...' His concluding shrug said the rest.

No use, so remove her. Sara found a small smile. 'I never wanted a nanny in the first place,' she remarked.

'You were ill,' he reminded her, getting up to go over to the internal telephone. 'Tea for my wife,' he ordered curtly to whoever it was who answered. 'And whatever she usually eats for breakfast.

'You needed help with the child,' he continued as he returned to his seat.

That filled her eyes with a rueful wryness that rid them of a little bit of strain. 'Have I managed to make a single move during the last three years that you don't know about?' she mocked, not expecting an answer—and not getting one.

She knew how Nicolas worked. 'What's mine I keep,' et cetera. And that was exactly what he had done over the last three years—kept his wife and her child in the kind of comfort that would be expected of a man of his stature.

So when Sara had gone down with a severe bout of flu several months ago Julie, the nanny, had appeared to take over caring for Lia. Since then, she'd stayed, not by Sara's request but probably because this man had ordained it so. Now the nanny had been banished again. For being of no use. For falling into a fit of hysterics in the park instead of responding as she should have responded when her charge was snatched from right beneath her nose and coming straight home to inform Lucas, the chauffeur, who would have then immediately informed Nicolas, his boss—probably before he would have informed Sara. Because Lucas the chauffeur was not just a chauffeur. He was Sara's guard, and she chose the word selectively. Lucas was paid to guard one of Nicolas Santino's possessions, namely his wife—not the child, who he did not believe was his child and therefore did not warrant her own guard to watch her every move. Which was why someone had managed to take her.

The breakfast-room door opened and Mrs Hobbit came in carrying a tray loaded with tea things and some lightly toasted wholemeal bread. She smiled nervously at Nicolas and warmly at Sara.

'Now, you eat this toast,' she commanded sternly, her busy hands emptying the tray onto the table in front of Sara. 'Or I shall just follow you around with it until you do.'

'I will,' Sara whispered, her eyes filling with a sudden burst of weak tears at the older woman's rough kind of affection. 'Thank you.'

'Oh!' the housekeeper exclaimed in dismay when she saw the tears. And suddenly Sara was being engulfed by a big, homely bosom. 'Now, there, there,' Mrs Hobbit murmured soothingly. 'You need a good cry, and don't we all?' Her soft bosom quivered on a sigh. 'But the little princess will be back here before you know it, all safe and sound; you wait and see.'

'Yes. Of course.' With a mammoth drag on her energy, Sara pulled herself together, straightening out of the older woman's arms. 'I'm sorry. It was just...' Her words trailed off, lost in the helplessness she was feeling inside.

'I know exactly what it was,' Mrs Hobbit said grimly. 'You don't have to explain anything to me, madam. Not a thing...'

With that she patted Sara's arm and walked out, leaving Sara alone with a very still Nicolas who had observed the whole exchange without uttering a single word.

Sara didn't look at him—couldn't. She had an idea that he had been rather shocked by Mrs Hobbit's affectionate display.

'They all—care for you a great deal, don't they?' he commented at last. 'I've already had Lucas in this morning enquiring about how you are coping. And Mr Hobbit stopped me in the garden earlier to do the same.'

Was he making a comparison with the cold, stiff way his Sicilian servants had treated her? He should do. The difference was palpable. 'Surprised, are you?' she countered drily, reaching out with an unsteady hand for the teapot. 'That anyone could care for the likes of me?'

To her surprise he got up and stepped tensely over to the window. 'No,' he replied, the single negative raking over a throat that sounded usually dry for him.

A silence fell, and Sara poured herself a cup of tea then cupped it in her fingers, bringing it to her lips to sip lightly at the steaming hot drink. He didn't turn back to the table, and they remained like that for long, taut minutes, she sipping at her drink, he lost inside some tense part of himself.

'Is she?' he asked suddenly. 'A little princess?'

Sara stared at his long, straight back and felt the bitter burn of a bloody anger begin to swell inside her. Today he had the damned effrontery to ask a question like that when only last night he had virtually denied her the right to so much as speak of the child! He had even tossed the baby's picture away from him in open distaste!

She stood up, discarding her cup onto its saucer with the same appearance of distaste. 'Go to hell, Nicolas,' she said, and walked out of the room.

The morning stretched out like an interminable wasteland in front of her, growing more difficult to bear the longer it went on without a single telephone ringing in the house. The silence grated. The sense of utter, wretched helplessness grated. The way everyone else seemed to be getting on with their normal business grated. And the burning fact that Nicolas had locked himself away in the study and not come out again grated. Because he should be right here by her side comforting and supporting her! Worrying with her!

If he truly believed Lia to be his daughter would he be so calm and collected about it all? Would he be sitting in that damned study getting on with the day's business while the people who had stolen their baby decided to make them sweat with this long, cruel silence?

In the end, she couldn't stand it. Couldn't stand any of it any longer. In an act of desperation she ran upstairs, dragged on an old pair of washed-out and skin-tight jeans and a T-shirt and ran downstairs again, busily tying a dark green cotton apron about her slender waist while trying to open the front door at the same time.

'Can I help you, Mrs Santino?' A big, burly body-guard stepped out in front of her.

'No,' she said. 'Thank you.' And she went to walk past him.

The big hand closing quite gently around her arm made her freeze. 'Take your hand off me,' she instructed him glacially.

A dark flush rushed into his face. But he maintained his grip on her arm. 'I have instructions that you are not to—'

'Nicolas!' she shouted at the top of her voice.

Doors flew open all over the place—including the study door. Nicolas appeared in the hallway, his gaze sharp-eyed and questioning as he took in the little scene being enacted on the steps of the front porch.

'Tell him,' Sara breathed, barely enunciating because of the revulsion bubbling inside her, 'to get his hands off me!'

Instead of obeying, Nicolas frowned. 'What is this, Sara?' he asked in genuine puzzlement. 'You must know that none of my men mean you any harm—'

'Tell him,' she repeated, her quivering mouth ringed by a white line of tension. '*Tell him right now!*'

His face darkened, his walk as he came down the hall towards her a statement in itself. He wasn't used to being spoken to like that, especially in front of his lackeys. And he did not like it that she was daring to do so now.

He flashed the guard a slicing look that had him ab-ruptly letting go of her arm then melting away like ice on hot coals. 'Right,' he said shortly. 'Would you like to tell me what that was all about?'

'No,' she replied, her face still tense with anger and disgust.

He wouldn't understand if she did try to explain how no man—no man—would ever touch her again without her permission—not without her retaliating accordingly, anyway. She had learned that lesson the hard way, at Jason Castell's hands. If she had screamed then, if she'd only had the sense to scream and shout and make loud protests, then Nicolas would have known she deserved his help and not his anger. And everything else would have been so different.

He sighed, his whole manner impatient. 'Then would you like to tell me where you think you are going?'

'Out,' she said. 'Or am I under some kind of house arrest?' she then asked bitterly.

'No.' He denied that, but in a way that only helped to irk her further. 'But I would have thought your daughter's plight was more important to you than any appointment you may desire to keep.'

Sarcasm, dry and deriding. She responded to it like a match to dry wood. 'Don't you dare try telling me what should be important to me,' she flashed, 'when you have no understanding of the concept yourself!'

An eyebrow arched, black, sleek and threatening, golden eyes warning her to watch her step. 'Where do you think you are going, Sara?' he repeated smoothly.

'I don't think it, I know it!' she asserted. 'We still have the right of free will in this country in case you didn't know it. I can go where I please without answering to anyone and that includes you and your damned henchmen!'

With that she turned, hair flying out in a silken fan of sun-kissed gold, the frustration that had been building up all morning culminating in that one furious movement.

His hand circling her wrist halted her mid-step, pulling her back round to face him. 'Stop it,' he commanded when she tried to tug free. His face was dark, its angles sharpened with anger. 'Now try again,' he suggested. 'And this time come up with a suitable reply. Where do you think you are going?' He enunciated it warningly.

She glared into his predator's eyes, glared down at the place where his long fingers were crushing the bones in her slender wrist, felt the ready tears burst into her eyes and the frustration alter to despair. Felt horrid and frightened and useless and fed up and lonely and—

'To help Mr Hobbit in the garden,' she whispered thickly, and wilted like a rag doll. 'Where else would I be going dressed like this?'

He should have recognised what she was wearing! He might hate the very sight of her, and he might have come to despise her lack of sophistication and good dress sense. But did he really think she would go out into the street dressed like this?

And he really should have recognised the apron as the same kind she always wore to work in the garden!

And it hurt—hurt like hell that he hadn't.

He muttered something. What, she didn't catch, because she was too busy fighting the onset of tears. Then the grip on her wrist slackened and she slid it free to lift it into her other hand where she rubbed at it pitiably.

'Where are your gloves?' he enquired gruffly.

So, he remembered that she usually wore gloves to protect her hands! One small tick in his favour, she thought sarcastically, and indicated with a half-nod of her bowed head towards the side of the house. 'In the garden shed,' she mumbled.

'Come on, then.' His arm coming to rest across her shoulders made her stiffen in rejection, but he ignored it. 'Let's go and find your gloves.'

She went with him simply because he gave her no choice, the arm remaining where it was as they walked together around the front of the house to the side where, cleverly concealed behind a high box hedge, the big garden shed stood with its door open to reveal the multitude of gardening implements held inside.

The moment they reached it, she went to move away from him, but he stopped her, the arm remaining firm as he twisted his body until he was standing in front of her. Then he reached out to pick up her wrist—the wrist he had used to pull her back towards him. His fingers were gentle as they ran over the tiny marks already promising to become bruises in the near future.

Sara kept her face lowered and didn't even breathe. If she did breathe she would weep; she knew she would. She was feeling so raw at the moment that anything— anything—was likely to set her off.

'I'm sorry,' he said eventually. 'I'm sorry if I over-reacted. But you must understand that it is not safe for you to come outside without someone with you. And I am sorry for this.' His thumb brushed a gentle caress over the fine veins in her wrist. 'I forgot my own strength, and the delicacy of yours.'

'Why isn't it safe?' she asked huskily.

He didn't answer for a moment, then gave a small sigh. 'We're dealing with ruthless people here, Sara,' he said grimly. 'They will stop at nothing to get what they want. Which means they would very much like to snatch you too if they thought they could get you.'

'Why?' She lifted tear-filled eyes to him in wretched bewilderment. 'Isn't it enough that they have my baby? What more do they think another life is worth on top of hers?'

For the first time since he had walked back into her life yesterday, she saw the Nicolas she used to know. The one who didn't slice her in two with his eyes. The one who looked almost—tender.

A tenderness that was mirrored in the way he dropped her wrist in favour of stroking a gentle finger over her pale cheek. 'When I married you I went against my father's wishes,' he reminded her. 'In their eyes that makes you my most prized possession.' He paused, looking deeply into her hollowed, anxious eyes which showed such a complete lack of comprehension, then sighed heavily. 'The child is enough. They know she is enough, but in case I decide not to toe the line some extra leverage would suit them down to the ground.'

'But you are toeing the line, aren't you?' she demanded with an upsurge of alarm. 'You won't put her life at risk by playing games with them?'

His eyes flashed, tenderness wiped out by anger. 'What do you think I am?' he muttered. 'Some unfeeling monster? Of course I won't put her at risk!'

'Then why are you trying to frighten me with all this talk of my own safety being at risk?'

'Because they have already threatened it, dammit!' he growled, then pulled her to him—as if he couldn't help himself, he pulled her to him and pressed her face into his chest. 'I shall kill them if they so much as touch you,' he vowed harshly. 'Kill every single one of them!'

'But you don't feel the same killer instinct for the baby,' she noted, and firmly pushed herself away from him.

He sighed, derision cutting an ugly line into his mouth. 'Is it not enough for you that I can feel that kind of emotion for a faithless wife?' he mocked himself bitterly.

'No,' she replied. 'It isn't enough.' And she walked into the garden shed and away from him.

He followed her, his expression harsh to say the least. 'You give no quarter, do you?' he rasped.

'No,' she agreed, rummaging through the mad clutter that decorated the workbench. 'Why should I, when you gave none to me?'

'I kept you, Sara,' he seared, 'when I should have thrown both you and your child out on the street to starve!'

'And why didn't you?' she challenged him, spinning to face him. 'Because you were protecting your own pride, Nicolas,' she offered as the answer. 'That isn't giving anything,' she declared. 'That is just you protecting you.' With a gesture of contempt, she turned back to the bench. 'So if you're expecting eternal gratitude forget it. You did me no favours allowing me to stay here, and if anything I hold you responsible for not protecting us properly when you must have known we were at risk!'

His response to that was a short, hard, mocking laugh. 'You are amazing, do you know that?' he said in scathing disbelief. 'It is no wonder you remain so stunningly beautiful when you can shed blame as easily as you do! Your own sins are not allowed to linger long enough to place a single line of guilt or shame upon your lovely face! It must be the perfect recipe for eternal youth!'

'And what's your recipe?' she countered, then went very still, realising what she had just said.

He was still too, silent, unbreathing, pumping the wretched Freudian slip for all it was worth. Then, 'For my beauty?' he prompted silkily.

Her nerve-ends went into panic mode, forcing her hands to move again in short, jerky movements. 'Men aren't generally described as beautiful.' She dismissed his question as casually as she could.

But it was too late. She'd known it was too late from the moment she let the foolish remark slip from her lips. He was suddenly standing right behind her, bending to brace his hands on the bench at either side of her tense frame, his breath warm against her slowly colouring cheek. 'Yet beautiful was always the word you used to describe me,' he reminded her softly. 'You would lie naked on top of me with your lovely hair caressing my shoulders and your slender arms braced on my chest. You would look into my eyes and say with heart-rending solemnity, ''You are so beautiful, Nicolas,''' he chanted tauntingly.

'Stop it,' she hissed, having to close her eyes to blot out the picture he was so cruelly building. But it wouldn't be blocked out. Instead it played itself across the backs of her quivering eyelids. Beautiful hair... She could hear herself saying it in that soft, adoring voice she used to use as her fingertips had reverently touched the smooth black silk. Beautiful nose, beautiful mouth, beautiful skin...

And he used to listen—listen to every shy, soft, serious word with a solemn intensity that made her sure, so sure, that the moment had touched something very deep inside him.

You have beautiful shoulders . . . Her fingers would trace them, sliding lovingly over the muscular curves and hollows. Beautiful chest . . .

She let out a shaky sigh, her tongue sneaking out to run a moistening caress around her suddenly dry lips because she knew what her mind was going to conjure up next. And it conjured up the way her head would lower, her soft mouth closing round one of his beautiful, taut male nipples . . .

His response had been that of a man driven beyond anything, his eyes turning molten, the breath escaping his lungs on a harshly sensuous rasp. And in a quick, sure, purely masculine action he would lift his legs to clamp them around her slender hips then tug her downwards—down until she—

'Did you whisper those same soft, evocative words to your lover?'

The angry growl had her eyes flicking open, her whole body jumping on a sudden stinging crack back to reality. His hands came up, hard on her shoulders, to spin her around.

'Did they have the same mind-blowing effect on him they used to have on me?'

She shook her head, unable to answer, white-faced and pained, her breasts heaving on a single frightened intake of air when she saw the anger scored into his face—the hard, murderous jealousy.

'Have you any idea what it did to me imagining you lying there with him like that?' he grated. 'I loved you, dammit!' he snarled. 'I worshipped the very ground you stood upon! You were mine—mine!' He shook her hard. 'I found you! I woke you! I *owned* this beautiful body and those beautiful words!'

'And I never gave either to anyone else!' she cried.

'Liar,' he breathed, and dropped his mouth down to her own.

It was punishment. It wasn't meant to be anything else. His lips crushed hers back against her clenched teeth until, on a strangled gasp, she gave in to the pressure and opened her mouth. From then on it was both a punishment and a revelation. A terrible, terrible revelation because from the moment their tongues met all sense of now went flying, and she found herself tossed back three years into a hot, throbbing world where this man reigned supreme. It was the smell of him, the taste, touch, texture.

Texture. The texture of his angry lips forcing her own apart, the texture of his moist tongue sliding against her own, the texture of his smooth, tight cheek rubbing against the softness of hers, and there was the sensation of his breath mingling with hers, and the drowningly sensual sound of his groan as she gave into it all and buried her fingers in his hair, pulling him closer, hungry, greedy for something she had not known she had been starving for until this bright, burning moment.

When he eventually wrenched himself away she sank weakly back against the bench behind her, unable to do anything but wilt there while her shattered senses tried to regroup.

The air inside the shed was hot and stifling, the sun beating down on the roof filling it with the musty smell of baking wood, old oil and earth.

He stood about a foot away, his breathing harsh and his body tense. Violence still skittered all around them, the threat of it dancing tauntingly in the motes of dust skittering in the musty air.

Then came the distinctive sound of a telephone, shattering the tension like glass. He raked his hand into his trouser pocket, came out with a small mobile telephone and pressed it to his ear.

'Right,' he gritted after listening for a moment. 'I'm on my way.'

'What?' Sara choked out, coming upright with an alarmed jerk.

He didn't answer. Did not even spare her a glance as he turned to walk out of the shed.

'Don't you dare shut me out as if I don't count!' Sara spat hoarsely after him. 'She is my child! *Mine!* If that was a call to say they are making contact again, then I have a right to know!'

His big shoulders flexed, the muscles bracing and stretching beneath the fine covering of his shirt. 'They are making contact,' he said, then walked off, out into the sunshine and away, leaving her standing there, trembling, wanting to throw something after him, wanting to scream, wanting to tear the whole world down!

'You bastard,' she whispered wretchedly. 'You cruel and unfeeling bastard.' Tears filled her eyes. 'Why can't you care? Why can't you care?'

She was sternly composed, though, by the time he opened the study door long, agonising minutes later to come to a sudden halt when he saw her sitting in a chair across the hall.

She looked like a schoolgirl who had been told to wait outside the headmaster's office, all big eyes and pensive uncertainty.

Only her mouth was not the mouth of a schoolgirl. Her mouth was the full, pulsing mouth of a woman. A woman who had recently been quite violently kissed.

She shot to her feet. 'Well?'

He shook his dark head. 'Nothing,' he said. 'It was a false alarm. A hoax caller.'

'H-hoax?' She mouthed the word in numb disbelief.

'We have had several of them.'

Her head twisted at that, the gesture sharp with pained disgust at a fellow human being who could be so cruel as to try to cash in on other people's anguish. She didn't say another word, but simply walked away, taking the stairs with her spine erect and her chin up.

Alone, as only a woman in her situation could be.

'She did that like a princess,' Toni Valetta remarked with quiet respect from Nicolas's side.

To his consternation the remark acted like a lighted fuse on a time bomb. The other man turned on him, his eyes sparking yellow murder. 'Go to hell,' he rasped, stepped back into the study and closed the door, right in Toni's surprised face.

If Toni Valetta had been present at the breakfast table that morning, he would have understood all of that. As it was, he stared blankly at the door, gave a bewildered shrug and walked away.

CHAPTER FIVE

THE afternoon dragged on interminably. Lunch, which Sara didn't even bother to turn up for, came and went. Then more hours, hours where she roamed from room to room, drifting out if someone else came in, wanting to be alone, needing to be alone because there was no one she could share her torment with.

Dinner that evening was another grim, silent affair, if only because none of them were prepared to pretend that there was anything even vaguely normal about it. Sara had joined Nicolas and Toni for the meal, but only because Nicolas had sent up a message to her room ordering her to attend, and she just didn't have it in her even to try to argue.

So she sat at the table, played lip-service to Mrs Hobbit's delicious chicken soup, cut up the light, fluffy omelette that must have been specially prepared to tempt her failed appetite because the other two were served thick, tender steaks, managed to swallow a couple of mouthfuls, accepted a glass of water, refused dessert and coffee then excused herself and left the two men to it without so much as uttering a single word except the pleases and thank-yous that good manners required.

'She can't take much more of this,' Toni grimly observed as the door closed behind her.

Nicolas flashed him a deadly glance. 'Do you think I am blind?' he gritted.

And that was that, the atmosphere at the table no better with Sara gone from it. They too finished their meal in silence.

A couple of hours later Nicolas Santino opened the door to Sara's bedroom to find the room empty. He frowned, eyes skimming over to the bathroom where the door stood open and its inner darkness told its own story.

He strode back down the stairs again and checked in every room before returning to the study where Toni sat at the desk with his eyes fixed on the television screen across the room. 'It's on the news,' he informed his employer. 'They're intimating Mafia connections and God knows what else. I thought you'd put a blackout on this.'

'I did.' He stepped further into the room. He had just taken a shower and had changed his clothes for buff cords and a fleecy cotton shirt. 'Has Sara been looking for me while I was showering?' he asked the other man.

'No,' Toni glanced up, frowning. 'Isn't she in her room?'

Nicolas didn't answer, his expression tightening. 'Get hold of whoever is running that bloody news station and put a block on it,' he commanded.

'A bit like locking the door after the horse has bolted, Nic,' Toni said drily.

'This whole thing is an illustration of that remark,' he clipped. 'She can't have got out of the house, could she?'

It took a moment for Toni's mind to swap subjects. 'Sara?' he said then. 'No chance. Alarm bells would have gone off, bringing ten men running and at least three dogs. And anyway, why would she want to go out?'

'I don't know,' Nicolas frowned. 'But she's not in her room and she's not in any room down here...'

Toni stood up, a mobile telephone suddenly stuck to his ear. 'I'll check with the men,' he said grimly. 'You check upstairs again.'

He went, taking the stairs two at a time then methodically opening doors and checking inside every room on the seven-bedroomed landing.

He found her in the last one—and would have missed her altogether if the shaft of light spilling in from the landing hadn't fallen on the flow of her long golden hair.

It made him still—several things made him still, but the fact that she was sitting on the floor curled up against the bars of a baby's cot had the severest effect on him, closing his lungs and tightening his chest when he realised that this was her child's room, and it was a child's pretty pink fur animal she was clutching to her breast.

Her eyes were open. She knew he was there. He had to swallow on a wave of black emotion that ripped at him inside—at his heart because of how utterly bereft she looked—and his anger stirred because he cared when he knew he should not.

'Don't put on the light,' she said when his hand reached out to do just that. 'Have they called again?'

'No.' Slowly he lowered his hand then leaned a shoulder against the doorframe. 'What are you doing in here, Sara?' he sighed out heavily. 'This can only be more painful for you.'

'It comforts me,' she said. 'I miss her. She's missing me.'

She didn't look comforted. She looked tormented.

'You need sleep,' he muttered.

'Lia won't sleep,' she countered dully. 'Not without Dandy.' Pulling the fluffy pink teddy from her breast, her fingers began gently smoothing its soft fur. 'He goes to bed with her every night. A nursery rhyme first, then a cuddle. Then she—'

'Come out of here!' he cut in harshly. Then when she went instantly quiet he added wearily, 'You are only punishing yourself doing this.'

But she didn't move, showed no sign at all that she'd even heard him, her fingers trailing gently over the satin-soft fur.

'Sara!' he bit out impatiently.

'No,' she said. 'Go away if you don't like it. But this is where I feel closest to my baby and this is where I'll stay.'

Toni came up behind him then, catching the huskily spoken words and the way muscles began to work all over his friend and employer's face. 'OK?' he said gruffly.

'Get lost, Toni,' Nicolas responded thickly, the very fact that once again he could speak to his best friend like that a revelation of what he was struggling with inside him.

Toni silently moved away, his handsome face carved in a grim mask of sympathy—whether for one or both of them he wasn't sure himself. Certainly, Sara deserved sympathy for what she was having to endure. But he hadn't expected to see Nic look so damned tormented by it.

Slowly Nicolas levered himself away from the door and came further into the room, releasing the light his frame had been blocking so he could see more clearly—the pretty pink walls dressed with baby pictures, white-painted shelves decked with baby toys. The carpet beneath his feet was pink, as were the curtains at the windows.

His face tightened and he moved stiffly to stand staring out at the still, dark night, pushing his hands into his trouser pockets.

Sara allowed herself to look at him. Look at this man whose lean, lithe body she had once known more intimately than she knew her own body. A man she had loved to just look at like this, to *feel* with that warm, dark sense that resided somewhere deep inside herself, the wonder of knowing that he belonged to her. This man, this—special man.

Hers. Just as unequivocally as she had been his.

He was eight years older than she and usually it showed. He used to like that, she recalled—like the way they contrasted with each other. Whereas he was dark she was fair, whereas he was hard she was soft, whereas he was cynical with worldly experience she was as innocent and naïve as a newborn babe.

They were complete opposites, he the tall, dark sophisticate with a cool maturity stamped into his lean features, she the small and delicate blonde whose youth and natural shyness made her vulnerable and therefore ignited his male need to protect.

He'd liked to have her at his side, to feel her hand clutching at one of his or resting in the crook of his arm, or simply to know that she needed to be standing close enough to touch him to feel at least bearably at ease in the élite kind of company he circulated in.

He had had the instincts of a killer shark in every other aspect of his life except where she was concerned; when he was with her his whole demeanour would soften so openly that it used to set other women's teeth on edge in envy of something she possessed that they knew they could never emulate.

An innate femininity, he'd called it—a certain fragile delicacy of mind, body and spirit that most women these days had polished out of them before they even left their cradles.

But its novelty value had worn off after a while, especially when the pressure of his workload had grown heavier by the week and she had not appeared to be learning to cope well without his being right beside her. Then the shyness that had originally drawn him towards her had become an irritant that he had, in the end, had little patience with. Adding to that the fact that she had been seriously afraid of his father, he had actually become angry with her when she'd begged him at least to let her set up house for them on their own.

'This is our home,' he'd stated. 'Is it not enough that you offend my father with your nervous attitude towards him without further insulting him by wanting to move out of this house?'

'But he doesn't like me.' She'd tried to make him understand. 'I'm not what he wanted for you, Nicolas, and he lets me know it at every opportunity he gets!'

'He teases you for your shyness, that's all. It is your own paranoia that makes you see everything he does as malicious!'

Which was just one display of his own blindness where Alfredo was concerned. For Alfredo had not been just malicious in his dealings with his son's unwanted wife, he had been downright destructive.

'OK,' Nicolas said gruffly now. 'Talk about it.'

The command made her blink, simply because she had been so lost inside her thoughts about him that she had forgotten he was actually there.

'About what?' she asked.

The profiled edges of his jaw flexed. 'The child,' he said. 'What you're feeling right now. Talk about it.'

Sara smiled wearily. 'You don't really want to hear.'

'If it helps you, I will listen.' He took a deep breath then let it out again. 'Tell me what she is like,' he invited in a low voice.

What was he thinking? she wondered curiously. What was he really thinking behind this—false façade of caring? Was he simply humouring her as his words suggested or was there something more profound going on here? Was Nicolas looking for an excuse for the right to care?

'You saw her picture. She looks like me,' she told him, wishing she could announce some clear physical evidence of the father who'd sired her child, but she couldn't. 'My features. My hair. My eyes . . .' She could have told him her daughter had her father's smile, his stubbornness, his ability to charm the socks off anyone. But it would not be enough, so she didn't say it. 'She was a late talker but an early walker. And she likes to be smiled at. If you frown at her she'll cry. She has done from—'

Her throat locked, choking her, because she had a sudden vision of those people who had taken her, frowning all the time and—

Oh, God. 'Nicolas,' she whispered starkly. 'I'm frightened.'

He turned, his eyes as dark as his expression. 'I know,' he acknowledged quietly.

'If they hurt my baby—' Again she stopped, having to struggle with the fear clawing at her insides. 'Would they hurt a baby?' Her eyes were dark with torment. '*Could* they hurt a baby?'

'Don't,' he sighed, but for once his voice sounded rough and unsteady, and the shoulders beneath the shirt flexed as if they could not cope with the tension attacking them. 'They will not hurt her,' he insisted. 'It will serve them no useful purpose to hurt her.'

'Then why this long silence?' She stared at him wretchedly. 'What are they waiting for?'

'It is a game they are playing with us,' he grimly replied. 'The cruel game of making us sweat. They do it to push up the ante, so that by the time they do call again we will be so out of our heads that we will agree to anything.'

'And will you—agree to anything?'

'Oh, God,' he rasped, his fingers going up to rub at his aching eyes. 'How many times do I have to tell you that I will do whatever is in my power to get your child back?' He turned on her angrily.

Remorse brought tears brimming into her eyes. 'I'm so sorry,' she whispered. 'But it's just all so . . .'

His harsh sigh eased her of the need to finish. 'Come on,' he said, and bent to lift her firmly to her feet. 'You are exhausted; you need rest which you will not get here.'

He was right; she was so tired that she could barely stand on her own, but she pleaded with him, 'Don't send me back to that bedroom. Please! I feel so alone there!'

'You will not be alone.' Grimly, he plucked the pink teddy from her fingers, then laid it back in the cot. 'For I shall be with you.'

'You?' She frowned in surprised confusion. 'But—'

'I will brook no protest from you, Sara,' he cut in warningly. 'You need rest. I am offering you the physical comfort of my presence. The alternative is two sleeping tablets the doctor left for just such a contingency. The choice is yours. Make it, but make it quickly or I will do it for you.'

Her luminous eyes lifted to search his, trying to discover why he was suddenly being like this. His own lashes lowered, two arcs of black settling against his cheekbones to hide what was going on in his head.

Something happened inside her—a soft flutter of yearning. A need. A memory of a time when this man had been as gentle and caring as any woman could wish for.

'You wish me to make this decision?' he prompted, at her continuing silence.

'Your accent is thickening,' she remarked, quite out of context.

He looked nonplussed momentarily, then grimaced. 'That is because I am as tired as you are,' he sighed. And in an act of failing patience he bent and lifted her into his arms. 'Your time is up,' he muttered, moving out of the baby's room and down the hallway to her own room. 'The decision is taken from you.'

He walked to the bed and allowed her bare feet to slide to the floor. Then he was grimly dealing with her robe, drawing it from her shoulders and tossing it aside to reveal a matching gown of the smoothest coffee satin, before leaning past her to flick back the covers on the bed.

'In,' he commanded.

Meekly, she did as she was told, while he turned his attention to extracting his mobile phone from his trouser pocket.

'Toni?' His voice was curt, demanding attention, not responses. 'I am with Sara. Disturb me only when it is time.' Click. The mobile was flicked shut.

'What did that mean?' she asked sharply, her wide eyes watching every move he made as he placed the mobile on the bedside table.

'Nothing,' he dismissed. 'I am expecting a call from New York.'

He began striding around the room, turning off table lamps until only the small silk-shaded one by the bed remained illuminated. Then he returned to the side of the bed, and, never once glancing at Sara, though she was sure he was aware that she never took her eyes off him, he discarded his shoes then stretched out beside her.

'Nic—' she began pensively.

'Shush,' he cut in. 'Go to sleep.'

'I was only going to say—thank you,' she whispered.

He didn't reply, didn't move, didn't do anything but lie there staring at the ceiling above their heads. Sara watched him do it, watched until her eyes began to sting and her lids grew heavy, watched until she could no longer watch, and at last drifted into sleep.

He was still lying there over an hour later, but had moved onto his side and was half dozing when she suddenly groaned and moved restlessly, throwing off the covers and twisting out of them so that she could curl herself against him instead.

'Nic,' she whispered, then placed her warm lips against his.

It was his downfall. He knew it and despised himself for it even as he gave in to it.

But she tasted so sweet. So exquisitely sweet. Like nothing he had ever tasted anywhere else in his life but from her . . .

It was wonderful. Like floating on a soft, fluffy cloud of rich, warm euphoria. Her body felt as light as a feather but her limbs were heavy, somnolent with the most honeyed delight. And her flesh was smiling. Could flesh smile? she asked herself wonderingly. Because hers certainly was. And since this was her dream she could let herself do and feel anything she liked. So, yes, her flesh was smiling, its outermost layer caressed by something warm and moist and infinitely pleasing.

She tried breathing not fast but slowly, savouring the sensual pull of oxygen into her lungs which seemed to set off a chain reaction throughout her body, setting her senses pulsing, slow and easy like the cloud she was floating on, the smile on her flesh, the sigh she released as she exhaled again.

'Nic,' she whispered.

That was what this was. It reminded her of Nicolas in one of his lazy, loving moods when he would lick her skin from toes to fingertips, raising a million and one sensations of pleasure all over her, rendering her lost and helpless. His to do with as he pleased.

'Sweet,' a hushed voice suggested.

Oh, God, yes, this was sweet, she agreed silently. The sweetest, sweetest sensation on earth—or in heaven. For she wasn't of this world right now. She was floating somewhere above it, stretched out, naked and basking, basking in the wonder of herself.

Her breasts felt full and heavy, her nipples stinging with impatience because he hadn't reached them yet. And they wanted him to. They wanted him to close his mouth around them, lick and suck and make them his own.

'Nic,' she whispered again, in breathless need this time.

'Shush,' the hushed voice answered.

She sighed in lazy agreement—then came fully awake with a muscle-locking, bone-clenching jerk when he slid the tip of his tongue into the delicate crevice between her thighs.

'Oh, God,' she gasped. 'Nicolas— No!'

'Yes.' He was suddenly looming over her, his face dark with passion, mouth full and moist from the havoc he had just been creating with his tongue.

And they were both naked! Her nightdress was gone— his clothes!—the crisp hair on his chest rasping against her breasts, one wonderfully muscular thigh heavy across her own.

'You want me, Sara,' he insisted. 'Your body wants me. Your subconscious mind wants me! Don't tell me no when I can feel you literally throbbing with need of me!'

'You said comfort,' she reminded him whimperingly.

'This is comfort,' he declared. 'The most exquisite comfort there is.'

'But—'

'No,' he gritted. 'I need this too! We both do.' Then he cut off any more protests with the hungry crush of his mouth.

She let out a single helpless sigh. He answered it by groaning something in his throat, then his tongue was playing with hers in the most sensuously evocative way, which brought her hands up to grasp tightly at his neck. His thigh moved against hers, rubbing a caress over the soft golden mound which protected her sex. His fingers trailed over her shoulders, her upper arms, then finally, exquisitely, her breasts.

'Do you know how sweet to taste you are?' he muttered, head coming up, hunter's eyes glowing at her in the darkness. 'How your skin secretes something onto my tongue that causes a chemical reaction inside me that drives me half-insane?' He sighed, as if he despised himself for saying all of that. 'I am addicted to you,' he admitted thickly. 'You are a fix I can get from no other source!'

'You've tried?' she asked painfully.

'Of course I have tried!' he admitted. 'Do you think I like feeling this way about you?'

'No,' she sighed on a wave of dark sadness for this man with his monumental pride which must be taking a battering because he had discovered he could not lie with her without wanting her. Wanting the woman he believed had betrayed him. 'I'm sorry,' she whispered. Sorry that fate had forced him to feel that way.

'Don't talk,' he commanded bleakly. 'I have to remember what you are when you talk. And I need this—*need it!*' he repeated hoarsely.

Then he groaned again, caught her mouth in a mind-blowing desperate kiss that brought tears to her eyes and her hands down to stroke his chest in a lame gesture of comfort to relieve his agony.

It was at that moment that she realised how much she still loved him, loved this man who could believe such vile things about her yet could still desire her as desperately as this.

The rest took place in a charged kind of silence, he arousing her with a grim sense of determination that told her he wanted the full collapse of all her senses before he would feel satisfied in taking her.

When he did eventually come into her, he did it with a ruthless precision that brought a grunt from his throat and a gasp from hers. Then he stopped, elbows braced at each side of her, eyes closing on a tense sideways jerk of his head that was in itself a dead give-away of how close he had driven himself to the edge before allowing himself to do this.

He filled her. In that moment of complete stillness Sara lay there and felt him fill her, felt the wonder of it, the beauty, felt her own muscles close around him, draw him deeper, hold him, knead him.

'Breathe,' he gritted. 'Damn you, Sara. Breathe!'

It was only as she sucked air into her lungs on a greedy gasp that she realised she had stopped breathing, her whole body locked in a spasm of sheer sensual ecstasy.

Her hands flew out, wildly uncoordinated as they searched for something solid to hold onto. They found his shoulders. He growled something in his throat, then his body was moving, thrusting—short, tense, blunt thrusts that held his face locked in a mask of total sexual compulsion and drove her over the edge to complete oblivion.

When she eventually dragged herself back from wherever she had gone off to, Nicolas was no longer in the bed. He was standing by it, pulling on his trousers with terse, angry movements, every cell in him sending out a message of bitter regret.

'Hating yourself now, Nicolas?' she taunted lazily.

He went still, then jerked his head round to look at her, the hunter's gold eyes barely brushing over her before they were flicking away again. 'Yes,' he answered flatly.

He didn't even have the decency to deny it, and that hurt. 'You seduced me,' she reminded him. 'It was not the other way round.'

'I know it.' Snatching up his shirt, he tugged it on. 'I am not blaming you for my own—'

He didn't finish. His jaw flexing with tension, he pushed buttons into holes. Sara watched him, too spent to do much else as he dropped into a chair to pull on socks and shoes. That done, he stood up, glanced at her then away again, as if he couldn't stand looking at her lying there like that, with her eyes languid and her body wearing the flush of a woman who had just been devoured.

'Will you be—all right?' he asked stiffly. 'If I leave you?'

Desperate to get away now he had disgraced himself? she wondered.

'Without you to *comfort* me, you mean?' she mocked. 'Yes, I'm sure I shall manage,' Her sarcasm bit. 'I'm used to being alone, after all,' she added bleakly. 'I've been alone since I was thirteen.'

'Not always,' he grited. 'Once, until you spoiled it, you had me.'

'Really?' She sliced a glance at him, his bitterness igniting her bitterness, and she scrambled off the bed to reach angrily for her robe. She didn't even care that she was exposing her body to him. Nicolas hated himself for desiring her, so let him gaze at her naked body—and hate!

'Alone, Nicolas,' she repeated. 'Even with you. You gave me no support, no rights. No say in how we ran our marriage. If I dared to object, you shut me up in the most effective way you knew how.' She meant in bed, and he knew it; his grim mouth tightened. 'If I persisted, you shot me down with hard words and derision. You thought it amusing that I liked to be amongst flowers rather than people, but never once allowed me the concession that maybe I had a right to like what I wanted to like no matter how empty-headed and frivolous it seemed to you.'

'I never considered you empty-headed,' he muttered.

'You rarely considered me at all,' she countered, searching angrily around her for the tie to her robe. 'Except where it mattered exclusively to you. Then I was expected to put up and shut up, because you knew best and I was, after all, just the pretty little doll you'd had the grace to elevate onto such an exalted plateau in life! Your servants rated higher in the pecking order than I did. They—' she pulled the belt tight around her waist '—looked down on me!'

He let out a short laugh, as if he couldn't quite believe he was hearing all of this. 'I don't know whether to weep for you or applaud you for stringing together more words than I've ever heard you manage in one go before!'

'Oh, applaud, Nicolas,' she flashed. 'I deserve the applause for putting up with it all for as long as I actually did!'

He turned away, the movement dismissive. 'You are beginning to bore me.'

'Well, what's new?' she retorted. 'You were bored with me within weeks of marrying me when you discovered I was going to be just a little more trouble than you thought I was worth! But I'll tell you something, Nicolas,' she continued hotly. 'If you grew bored with the shy, timid little mouse you married in a fit of madness, then I certainly grew tired of the tall, dark, handsome god I found myself tied to, because he turned out to be just one of a very select, very well cared for but boringly similar flock of sheep!

'Oh, their coats were exquisite,' she railed on recklessly, 'and they ate off the very best turf, but what they gained in fine finish they lost in good brain cells! They did the same things. They thought the same things. And they bleated on and on about the same things! Genetic farming, I think they call it. I had no idea it went on in human society as well as—'

'Have you quite finished?' he inserted coldly.

She nodded. 'Yes.' She felt flushed and breathless, incredibly elated. In all her twenty-five years she had never spoken to anyone like that. It had been almost as good as the sex!

'Then I shall remove my—genetic abomination from your presence,' he said, giving her a stiff, cold bow that was as big an insult as the way he had hated himself for touching her again.

'After I have said one last thing,' she threw at his retreating back. 'Make a note of today's date, Nicolas. For I took no precautions against what we just did in that bed over there, and I know for a fact that the idea just would not even enter your head! If I am pregnant because of tonight, I want there to be no doubt this time who the father of my child could be.'

He'd reached the door, from which he turned to slice her with a coldly shrivelling look. 'A genetic mutation?' he clipped out curtly. 'What an appalling thought.'

Shot down. With one smooth, clever one-liner, he had managed to turn her wild tirade back on her. She didn't know whether she wanted to scream or weep in bitter, blinding frustration!

What she actually did was sit on the edge of the bed and just—wilt.

CHAPTER SIX

BY THE time Nicolas got downstairs he was back to being the man most people knew him to be. He entered the study to find it a veritable Aladdin's cave of hi-tech equipment. Toni, the two policemen, two men he did not recognise but knew came from some special services department—all of them stood or sat about messing with the complicated array of communications stuff.

Stone-faced, hard-eyed, he homed directly in on Toni. Not by so much as a flicker of an eyelash did Toni's face reveal what he must be thinking, knowing how long Nicolas had been with Sara. 'Almost time,' he said quietly. 'Everything is ready.'

Nicolas gave a curt nod and moved over to the desk. The others in the room watched him like wary cats following the hunting pace of a dangerous animal. They were split into three groups—one group tracing, one group talking, one man ready to hit a command the moment they were given the go-ahead.

He sat down. 'Any problems?' he clipped.

'No.' It was Toni who answered. 'We have them pinned down to a certain area code, but to be sure this works we need more time.'

'It has to work,' Nicolas said grimly. 'Failure means panic and panic means risk. I won't have the child's life put at risk—you understand?' It wasn't said to Toni but to the two special agents huddled in a corner across the room.

The phone on the desk began to ring. The room froze into total stillness. Nicolas sat very still in his chair, hands tense, eyes fixed on the two policemen. And waited.

Two rings. Three rings. Four. He got the nod. He snatched up the phone.

'Ah, good evening, *signore*.' The smooth, oily voice slid snake-like into every headphoned ear listening in. 'You have resolved the small cash-flow problem, I hope. . .'

Dawn was just breaking the sky when Nicolas entered Sara's room and gently shook her awake.

She sat up with a jerk. 'What's happened?' she gasped, instantly alert, her eyes huge and frightened in her sleep-flushed face.

'It's over, *cara*,' he murmured soothingly. 'Your daughter is safe.'

'Safe?' She blinked up at him, not really taking the words in. 'Safe, Nicolas?' she repeated. 'Really safe?'

'Yes.' He nodded.

'Oh, God.' Her hand whipped up to cover her wobbling mouth, her eyes, still luminous with tears of relief. 'How. . .?' she whispered. 'Where is she?'

'I will take you to her just as soon as you can get dressed and be ready to travel,' he promised.

'She's not here?' Then in a burst of alarm she cried, 'Have they h-hurt her?'

'No, to both questions,' he answered calmingly. 'Here—' He turned away, then turned back to push a cup of something hot into her hand. 'Drink this, then get dressed. I would like to leave here in half an hour. Can you be ready?'

'I. . . Y-yes, of course. . .' She was suffering from shock—a new kind of shock, the shock of deliverance from the pits of hell, which stopped her from asking the kind of questions she knew she should be asking.

'Good.' He nodded, then, turning, went quickly towards the door.

'Nic!' She stopped him, waiting for him to turn back to face her before saying huskily, 'Thank you.'

After what had happened between them the night before, there was a certain amount of irony in that. But he took it at its face value, his half-nod an acknowledgement before he was turning away again.

'Downstairs in half an hour,' he instructed, and left her alone.

She was showered, dressed and ready to leave by the specified time. Nicolas was waiting for her in the hallway. He watched her come down the stairs towards him, his eyes drifting over the simple lines of the sage-green linen trousers and cream shirt she was wearing beneath an off-white jacket. She wore no make-up—she rarely ever did. And her hair she had brushed quickly and secured back from her face with a padded green band.

Nothing fancy. Nothing couture. Like the Sara he had first met. She had reverted to that person of simple tastes the moment he'd had her banished here to his London residence. She wondered if he was making the same distinction as he watched her like that, unrevealingly, with his eyes narrowed, so that she could not read what was going on behind them. But she made no apology for her appearance. This was what she was. That other person had been fashioned like a piece of sculpture to suit the role it had been intended to play. A false role, fake like the life she had been forced to live and the marriage that should never have been.

He, by contrast, looked dynamic again, not in one of his handmade silk suits but a pair of tobacco-coloured linen trousers and a white roll-neck worn beneath a black linen jacket—Armani, she guessed, recalling that his casual wardrobe had held mainly that designer's name.

'Where's Toni?' she enquired as he led the way outside into an early summer morning.

'He has business of mine to attend to,' he answered coolly, opening the rear door of the Mercedes saloon standing with its engine running at the bottom of the steps.

She smiled to herself as she climbed into the car. Problem solved, so Toni's attention had been turned back to business. Then she wondered how long she was to be graced with Nicolas's company before he turned his attention to other things.

For the duration of this drive? she suggested to herself as the car took off with Nicolas seated beside her and the driver safely hidden behind a wall of tinted glass. Until he had efficiently delivered Lia into her arms? Or would he feel duty-bound to see them safely back home again and maybe even hang around long enough to make sure that the security surrounding them was tight enough for something like this not to happen again?

She shivered, the mere idea of it occurring again striking like a death knell right through her. 'How far away is she?' she asked. 'Will it take long to get there?'

His dark head had been resting against the soft, creamy leather headrest, his eyes closed. But when she turned the questions on him his long lashes flickered then lifted slowly to reveal sensually sleepy pupils surrounded by a sandstorm of energy. It caught at her breath, because that look was his sexually hungry hungry male look and—

No. She glanced away, refusing to so much as think of him in that dangerous mould. Never again after last night! And anyway, how could he be looking at her like that after what he had said?

'Quite far,' he murmured, answering his first question. 'A plane journey actually. She is in Sicily,' he finally tagged on.

'Sicily?' The shock of it showed in the momentary blank blue look she fixed on him. 'But how could she be in Sicily?'

'With good planning,' he drawled. 'How else?' She shivered. Her baby had been taken so far away from her and she had been helpless to stop it. 'But I've not brought anything with me for a journey this long! No change of clothes for me, or for Lia. And my passport, Nicolas.' She turned to him urgently. 'I haven't brought my passport with me—'

'I have it,' he said. 'I recovered it from the wall-safe. Packed for you too,' he added wryly, because it wasn't a job he was used to doing for anyone, not even himself.

'For both you and the child while you were still sleeping.'

He had been in her room? Walking around it, packing for her while she slept? The very idea did the strangest things to her, filled her with alarm and a shocking sense of—

'You opened my safe?' she protested, picking on that one intrusion because the other did not bear thinking about.

'My safe,' he corrected her. 'My home.'

But she ignored the jibe because another thought had suddenly struck her, one that held the breath trapped in her lungs. 'Where is she in Sicily?' she asked.

There was a small hesitation. Then, 'With my father,' he said, watching her narrowly.

Alfredo. She stiffened, all her muscles clenching. 'After all you said,' she breathed. 'He was behind it all, wasn't he? He's the one who did this to me!'

'Not to your child, I make note,' he drily observed. 'I can at least take comfort in the fact that you are not accusing my father of wanting to hurt a child.'

Her blue eyes flashed in a bitter contradiction of that final remark. 'If he has hurt her,' she warned, 'so help me, wheelchair or not, I shall see him dead.'

'A Sicilian emotion,' he noted, 'this desire you have developed for retribution. Do you think we may have taught you something after all?'

His lazy mockery was spiked, the glinting eyes full of a cold condescension entirely aimed at previous diatribes in which she had condemned everything Sicilian.

'You people taught me many things, Nicolas,' she threw back at him. 'Not least the rule of possession. "What's mine I keep"!' she quoted. 'And woe betide anyone who tries to lay a finger on a possession of mine, including your wonderful father, who is nothing but a—'

'Stop right there,' he inserted very softly.

She sucked in a breath of air, her heartbeat pounding in her head. But it was no use. The fact that he had actually managed to convince her that Alfredo had nothing to do with Lia's abduction only made this moment of truth more impossible to deal with.

'And you still protect him, don't you?' she derided bitterly. 'No matter how many dirty tricks he pulls on you, you still refuse to see what a nasty, cunning, evil man he is—even when the proof of it is shoved right under your very—'

His hand snaking round her neck and yanking her forcefully towards him stopped the words. 'Hold your tongue, you little shrew!' he rasped. 'Before I bite it off!'

'I hate and despise you!' she threw into his angry face.

'You were warned,' he muttered, and crushed his mouth down onto hers in a brutal kiss aimed at subduing all hint of defiance left in her.

Yet within the punishment was a dark, duplicitous intimacy that dragged pleasurably at her senses and took some fighting against to stop her from sinking greedily into the kiss.

She groaned instead, pretending he had hurt her.

'You asked for it,' he muttered as he drew away.

'I got it, didn't I?' she muttered in return, pulling shakily out of his arms.

'What surprises me,' he struck back cruelly, his hand shooting out to capture her wrist then holding onto it so they could both feel the way the blood was breaking speed records as it thundered through her veins, 'is how you were affected by it. Could it be that you're just a little in need of a man, Sara? Has the princess been locked up in her tower too long, and did last night's little—taster remind her of what she once craved?'

'Can you be so sure the tower has been locked?' she retaliated, refusing point-blank to let him diminish her as he used to so easily.

His eyes glinted. 'You're damned right I can,' he gritted. 'I've told you before: what's mine I keep. And I've kept you under surveillance enough to be sure no man has been near you.'

'Except for my gaoler,' she threw back at him deridingly. 'In the end even you—hate yourself though you do for it—couldn't keep your hands off me.'

'I have the legal right,' he declared. 'If not the moral one.'

'And the princess in the tower had the cunning to let down her hair for her secret lover to climb,' she hit back, reminding him of the old fairytale.

His eyes narrowed. She held her breath, aware that she was prodding a very temperamental animal here yet, strangely, unable to stop herself—finding it exhilarating almost.

Then, deflatingly, he dropped her wrist and relaxed. 'You have changed,' he observed. 'You would not have dared speak to me like this three years ago.'

'Oh, yes,' she agreed, subsiding angrily into the far corner of the seat. 'I've changed. Grown up. Grown tough. What did you expect me to do, Nicolas?' She flashed him a bitter look. 'Remain the same gullible fool I was when I first met you? The one who thought you loved me above all others and would stand by me whatever was thrown at me?'

'You were the one who took a lover to your bed,' he reminded her. 'Not I!'

'And you were the one who threw me to the hungry wolves then dared to be disgusted with me when I cried to you for help!'

He threw her a contemptuous look, the disgust as clear in his eyes now as it had been three years ago. 'I notice you don't deny the charge of adultery,' he jeered.

'What's the use,' she asked, 'when you refuse to believe me?'

'Believe what?' he derided. 'Your lies?'

'I never lied to you,' she asserted.

'Denying that swine's presence in your room was no lie, was it?'

'I never denied he was there,' she insisted. 'Only my acceptance of his presence.'

'I fail to see the difference.'

'And I refuse to discuss this with you now,' she countered coldly. 'Besides the fact that it comes three years too late, I find I no longer care what you think. My daughter is all that matters to me now, and she is all I want to think about.'

'My father did not steal your child, Sara,' he said grimly. 'He *recovered* her. Or, at least, he coordinated the whole thing so his people could. She is at this moment sleeping safely under his protection. And soon, very soon,' he warned gratingly, 'I shall make you eat every filthy, lying word you've spoken about him. Understand?'

She understood. Another vendetta. Another reason to punish her for being foolish enough to mess with his close-knit clan.

Nicolas could believe what he liked about his father but just the simple knowledge that her daughter was in Sicily with Alfredo told her just who had arranged for her to be there.

What worried Sara now was his reason for doing so.

The Santino private jet landed at midday at Catania airport then taxied over to the far side of the runway. Away from the terminal. Away from the people.

That was the power of the Santino name. They were met by a Customs official. Nicolas dealt with him, tiredness pulling at the lean contours of his face now, even though he had slept away the whole flight.

And despite the hostility still thrumming between them Sara experienced a sharp pang of pity. Forty-eight hours ago he had been in New York. Since then he had crossed the Atlantic, dealt with a very stressful crisis then flown another few thousand miles to get here.

'Let's go,' he instructed her, placing a hand at the base of her spine to urge her to precede him off the aircraft.

His touch sent a spray of tingling awareness skittering across the surface of her skin. She had discarded her jacket on entering the plane, and knew from past experience that the weather in Sicily would not require her to put it back on. But she wished she had now, wished she'd decided to roast in the jacket rather than suffer the sensation of his hand so close to her skin.

And it wasn't revulsion she was experiencing, not any more. In the few fraught hours she had been back in his company, her senses had been reintroduced to their lord and master! And, good grief, they were clamouring with excitement!

It was a lowering truth. And one she didn't live easily with. Could Nicolas have been right when he'd accused her of being starved of a man's touch?

She hoped not. She hoped this was only a brief reaction to the stress she had been living under. Because it was a pride-levelling concept to find herself still so violently physically attracted to the man who had hurt her so badly.

It was a perfect Sicilian day, the air hot and dry, the sun burning down from a perfect porcelain-blue sky.

A car was waiting—a white limousine shimmering in the sunlight. Nicolas saw her into it then sat beside her. They took off almost immediately, making for a pair of high, wire-fencing gates which were drawn open by two uniformed members of staff as they approached.

Neither Sara nor Nicolas spoke. Both were tense. Sara was readying herself for the moment when she would see her daughter again, impatient but oddly nervous with it. And there was Nicolas. She frowned as she stared out at the bright, shimmering coastline they were following. She didn't know how he was going to react to his first meeting with the child he saw as the living evidence of his wife's betrayal.

She saw the house the moment they rounded a bend in the twisting road. It stood on its own halfway up an acutely sloped bay. And her heart gave an odd pull of recognition as her gaze drifted over beautiful, white-painted, flower-strewn walls built on several terraced levels to hug the lush hillside all the way down to the tiny, silver-skirted beach.

Then suddenly it was gone as the car cut inland, not far but enough to take them through a tunnel of leaf-weighted trees towards the rear of the house. It was the only access unless you came by sea. A beautiful place, very private, idyllic. A high, whitewashed stone wall stood impenetrable behind the gnarled trunks of old fig trees, two royal-blue-painted solid wood doors cutting them in an arch twisted with bougainvillea heavy with paper-like vivid pink blooms.

The car stopped, gave a single blast of its horn. A small square porthole cut into the blue opened then closed again. The blue-painted doors swung open on well-oiled hinges. The car began moving slowly through them into a huge cobbled courtyard alive with colour, with the dappling shelter of several olive trees, with the delicate sprinkle of water from the simple fountain gushing water into a circular pond.

Sara heaved in a tense breath then held onto it. She sensed Nicolas's swift glance in her direction but ignored it. This beautiful place was the scene of all her nightmares, and she needed to concentrate if she was to hold on to her composure.

Lia, she told herself grimly. Just think of Lia.

The car stopped. The driver got out, stepping up to open her door. Her senses were assailed by the sweet scent of flowers and the crisp tang of fruit, the quietness, the sheer peace that enveloped her just another deception she had to do battle with.

The house from the back appeared quite humble when compared with its dramatic front—a mere single storey of long white wall with blue-painted shutters thrown back from small windows and a terracotta-tiled roof.

Twin blue doors stood open to offer a welcome. Sara gritted her teeth, tried to make her suddenly shaky legs move. A cicada sawed lazily, hidden somewhere in a tree. No other sound. Nothing. Her hand reached out, unconsciously searching for and locating another, warmer, stronger hand. It closed around her trembling fingers, but she was not really aware of it as she forced herself to move forwards through the doors into a cool square hallway where she paused for a moment while her eyes adjusted themselves to the dimmer light inside.

It was all so familiar. The beautiful paintings adorning the walls, the tasteful mix of dark, well-polished furniture, delicate ornaments, and vases of flowers.

And the stony-faced housekeeper standing a couple of yards inside the hall.

But no baby to greet her. She glanced at Nicolas, eyes questioning, anxious. He stepped forward and spoke in low tones to the housekeeper then turned to come and take hold of Sara's arm.

'Where—?' she jerked out tensely.

'This way,' he said, his face stiff. He began leading her across the entrance hall and through an archway that she knew led to one of several stone staircases.

The house was built on several levels. Here on the top floor were the more functional services like kitchens and garages and servant accommodation. Then came the formal reception rooms where the Santino family entertained. Next was the floor given over entirely to the Santino empire, with office suites with all the relevant state-of-the-art equipment to go with them. The next tier housed the family's private bedroom suites, followed by the guest suites and finally the less formal pool and recreational tier where you would find the only televisions in the whole place, and the garden terrace, which stepped downwards to the tiny pebbly beach below.

There were some two hundred steps in all from top terrace to beach. Sara had counted them once during one of her lonely periods while Nicolas had been away and his father had driven her outside to seek refuge from his constant hostility. But those two hundred steps were outside. Inside, each level had its own stairway worked in a dog-leg which took you from tier to tier.

And as Nicolas led the way down her legs began to wobble, memories she would have much preferred to keep at bay beginning to crowd her mind.

Memories of a beautiful suite of rooms with a huge, white-silk-draped canopied bed and a man lying naked and glossy brown against the pure white sheets. A man who loved to just lie there like that and watch her as she moved about the room, loved to watch her brush her hair and cream her skin and . . .

'Sara.'

She'd stopped. She hadn't realised she'd stopped until the sound of her name brought her jolting to the present. Her lashes fell then lifted again to reveal the glaze of pained reminiscence as she found the same man watching her.

The same man but not the same, she noted bleakly. The one who'd liked to watch her move about their bedroom had worn a look of lazy pleasure on his face. This one looked hard and cold and . . .

'This way,' he prompted.

He was standing by the stairway to the next level. She frowned in puzzlement. 'But . . .' Her hand wafted out in the vague direction of the bedrooms, her logic expecting Lia to be in one of those. Then it hit her, and if she had been up to it she would have smiled at her own stupidity. The next level contained the guest suites. Of course Lia would be there. She was not family. Just as Sara herself was no longer family—not in the true sense of the word anyway.

She followed him, her head lowered so he would not read the irony she made their way down to the next level, and here, as she had expected, Nicolas led the way to a suite of rooms, then paused by the door as if taking a moment to brace himself for what was to come.

So did Sara.

The door swung open, she stepped up beside him—then went perfectly still, heart, lungs, everything inside her crashing to a shuddering halt at the sight that met her eyes.

Across the room and to one side of the open plate-glass window which led outside was a man. His dark hair was peppered with more silver than she remembered, his once big frame radically diminished by the wheelchair he was sitting in.

But it was not just the man who held all her stunned attention. It was what he held in his arms.

Lying against his chest was a baby wearing nothing more than a disposable nappy and a white cotton vest. Her golden head was cushioned on his shoulder, her little arms clinging tightly to his neck.

Her eyes blurred out of focus then back again, the sight of her child—*her child!*—clinging to her worst enemy seeming to rock the very ground she stood upon.

Then the greying head was turning, the bright, hunter's gold eyes searching out and homing directly in on Sara's eyes. And the expression glowing in them froze the blood inside her veins.

It was possession, fierce and parental. And at last Sara began to understand what this had all been about.

The child. *Her child!*

In his illness, Alfredo Santino had seen his own mortality. He had seen himself dying without ever holding his own grandchild. It no longer mattered that the child was also Sara's child. He wanted. And what Alfredo Santino wanted he got, even if it meant stealing to get it. Even if it meant having the woman he hated most coming back into his life. He wanted Lia. And there was no longer a single doubt in Sara's mind that it had been Alfredo who had orchestrated her child's abduction.

'No!' Sheer instinct brought the thick denial bursting from her locked throat. And, almost stumbling in her haste, she went towards him, saw, with a horror that tightened like a steel clasp around her chest, his hands move on her baby in a convulsive act of ownership.

'She would accept comfort from no one else but me!' he exclaimed in glowing triumph as Sara reached him. 'See how she clings. See!'

'No,' Sara breathed again, denying it, denying his right to feel this way about her baby—as he had denied the little girl her right to know the love of her own father!

As if the baby sensed the closeness of her mother, she gave a shaky sigh against Alfredo's shoulder, bringing Sara's attention swerving back her way. And suddenly Alfredo was forgotten. Nicolas, still standing tense and silent in the doorway, was forgotten, everything was wiped clean out of her mind as she watched the head of golden curls lift and slowly turn. A deep frown shadowing her luminous eyes, her Cupid's-bow mouth cross and pouting, she looked up at her mother, released another unsteady sigh then simply stretched out an arm towards Sara.

Sara bent, lifted the baby from Alfredo, folded her to her, one set of fingers spreading across the little back, the others cupping the golden head. The baby curved herself, foetus-like, into her mother, head nuzzling into her throat, arms tucking in between Sara's breasts.

Then neither moved. Neither spoke. Neither wept. Sara simply stood there with her eyes closed and her face a complete and utter blank, the emotion she was experiencing so deep that none of it was left to show on her whitened face.

CHAPTER SEVEN

It was like witnessing the most spiritual communion life could offer. And no one privy to it could not be moved by the vision. Not Alfredo, who lowered his silvered head and shook it with a sharp, jerky motion that was almost pained. Not the thin, dark-haired woman standing quietly to one side of the room, whose eyes filled with aching tears. Not even Nicolas, still standing tensely in the open doorway, who had to close his eyes to block out the heart-wrenching vision.

The seconds ticked by. No one moved. Not Sara. Not the baby. Not father or son or strange woman or even the air in the room, it seemed, in those few fraught moments.

Then the small head lifted, still frowning, still cross as she fixed her mother with a condemning look. 'Not like airplanes,' she said.

Sara's legs went from beneath her. No warning. It was as if the sound of the child's voice acted like a spring on all the control she had been exerting on herself and she simply-uncoiled, release flowing through her as if liquid were replacing bone.

Alfredo saw it happen but even as he let out a warning gasp, one gnarled hand lifting instinctively towards mother and child, Nicolas was there, bursting out of his statue-like posture to dart behind her so that her slender body melted against his own instead of falling to the floor, his arms snaking around both mother and child in support while the tension in his face reached crisis proportions.

The baby lifted her frowning eyes from her mother's pale face and for the first time in her life fixed them on the rigid contours of her father's.

Luminous blue met with harshly frowning gold. And while Sara fought a battle with her shattered control another communication took place—one which brought a muffled choke from Alfredo and set his son's teeth gritting behind his tightly clamped lips.

For this child was undoubtedly Sara. Sara's soft golden hair. Sara's soft mouth. Sara's pale, delicate skin. Sara's huge, beautiful blue eyes.

No hint of Sicilian. Not even a hint of the dark-haired Englishman Sara had betrayed him with. The child looked like an angel when she should have been wearing the stamp of the devil.

His instinct was to snap right away from both of them. But although Sara was still holding the child it was his arms that were taking the child's weight, his body that was keeping the mother upright.

'Take the child—quickly!' he raked out in an effort to release some of the violent emotion rushing through him right now.

But his feelings must have shown in his face, because the child's mouth quivered, her eyes growing even bigger as they filled with frightened tears.

Then, 'More bad man!' she cried, reacting to both his hard expression and the rough words which must have reminded her of her kidnap. 'Stay with Mama!' Her arms clutched tightly at Sara's neck. 'No more bad man, Mama,' she sobbed. 'Grandpa said!'

Grandpa?

Sara's eyes flicked open. Nicolas tensed up behind her. 'What the hell . . .?' he muttered.

'She needed reassurance,' Alfredo defended himself.

'I gave it in the only way I could think of!'

Liar! Sara's eyes accused him, and on a burst of anger that flooded the strength right back into her limbs she pushed herself free of Nicolas's supporting arms, trembling for an entirely different reason now as her hand spread protectively over her baby's head and she flashed both Santino men a condemning look.

'You vile people,' she whispered tightly, then turned and walked away—out through the open window and onto the terrace where the clean fresh air did not hold the taint of Santino.

'Sara!' Nicolas's voice, harsh with command, brought her to a shuddering halt halfway across the terrace towards the steps. 'Where the hell do you think you are going?' he muttered, catching hold of her arm.

'Let go of me,' she whispered, seething with a bitter enmity she was finding it difficult to keep under wraps.

'Don't be foolish!' he snapped.

'But you saw him, Nicolas!' she choked, turning wretched eyes on him. 'He did it! He set all of this up for some selfish reason of his own! And—'

'Be silent!' he barked. 'I have warned you before not to repeat accusations like that!' He wasn't seeing, she realised in despair—he would never see his father for what he really was.

His hard tone brought Lia's head out of her mother's throat, huge blue eyes homing in on his angry face, and the Cupid's-bow mouth wobbled a second time, the first cry leaving her on a frightened wail. 'Bad man again!'

'Nicolas!' A reprimand for his impatience came from an unexpected source. 'You are frightening the *bambina*!' Alfredo's voice, coming from the open doorway, carried above Lia's growing wails while Sara stood quivering with fury at the very idea that her child—*any* child—should have experience of what was bad in a human being!

'My father is right,' Nicolas conceded tautly. 'We are upsetting the child.' His hand tightened on Sara's arm. 'Come back inside,' he urged, taking care not to let his eyes clash with the wide, wary ones of the little girl. 'We are all overwrought. Come back inside...'

His hand urged her forward; reluctantly she went, aware that at this moment she really had no choice. They were right—both men were right and their manner was upsetting Lia. The poor baby had been through enough; she did not need her mother's hostile attitude confusing her further. But as she reached Alfredo, sitting tensely in his chair in the open doorway, she paused, her hard gaze telling him that she knew what he had done, no matter that his son refused to see it.

The hunter's gold eyes flickered then shifted from her to the baby where they softened into a gentle smile, a long-fingered hand reaching out to catch and squeeze a plump baby hand. The little girl responded immediately to the smile, offering one of her own.

'Grandpa,' she said, and once again rocked the precarious control Sara was clinging to.

It was said so affectionately.

It affected Nicolas too, his fingers tightening on Sara's arm as he urged her forward. 'You're a fool, Nicolas,' she said thickly. 'You always have been where he is concerned.'

He ignored that, jaw clenching in grim dismissal of the remark. 'Sit down,' he commanded, almost pushing her into a nearby chair, then he clicked his fingers to bring an anxious-looking woman hurrying across the room. 'This is Fabia,' he said.

Keeping her eyes away from a stiff-faced Nicolas, Sara glanced at the woman, who smiled nervously and nodded her dark head in acknowledgement. She was not much older than Sara herself, but with the luxuriant black hair of a Sicilian and beautiful brown eyes.

'Fabia is here to attend to your needs,' he continued in that same cool voice. 'And she will begin by collecting your luggage...' With a nod at the other woman he sent her scurrying on her way. Then his attention was back on Sara. 'I suggest you take the next few minutes to compose yourself and reassure the child.' Lia had taken refuge by burying her face in her mother's throat again. 'Father...?' Without giving Sara a chance to reply, he turned with that same cool, authoritative voice to Alfredo who was still sitting in the open window. 'We need to talk.'

With that he walked off, with a surprisingly obedient Alfredo in tow, propelling himself by the use of the electronic controls of his wheelchair.

Silence prevailed. Lia lifted her face from its warm hiding place. 'Bad man gone?' she asked warily.

Sara leaned into the soft-cushioned back of the chair and gently cradled the baby to her. 'He isn't a bad man, Lia,' she murmured quietly. 'Just a . . .'. Confused one, was what she'd been about to say—which puzzled her because Nicolas had never been confused about anything in his whole life!

Life was black and white to him; confusion came in those little grey areas in between, which he did not acknowledge. Which was why their marriage had been such a difficult one, because Alfredo, knowing his son, had carefully clouded everything to do with Sara grey, causing confusion and misunderstanding all the way.

Just as he was doing again now, she realised with a small frown, and wished—wished she knew what the old man was up to this time, because every warning instinct she possessed told her he was definitely up to something dire.

What did he want? Her baby all to himself?

But he could not have Lia without making Nicolas believe himself to be the child's father. And making his son believe that would also make Nicolas question his belief in Sara's adultery. And once Nicolas did start questioning the truth would surely come out. Dared Alfredo risk it? Risk his son discovering just how ruthless his own father had been in his quest to rid him of his wife?

Or had he got some other, even more devious plan up his sleeve, one where he convinced Nicolas that Lia was indeed his child but by mere fluke rather than fidelity? Which would then lead to Nicolas claiming the child and dismissing the wife!

She began to tremble—tremble inside with a fear that came from experience in dealing with Alfredo.

Black and white. Nicolas dealt in black and white. The grey area in Alfredo's favour was that Sara would never be able to prove she did *not* take another man to her bed!

'*Signora?*' The enquiry brought her eyes flickering into focus. Fabia was standing by her chair, her smile warm.

'The *bambina*,' she prompted softly. 'She sleeps peacefully at last with her *mama's* arms around her.'

Asleep. Sara glanced down in surprise to find that Lia was indeed fast asleep, her body heavy and her limbs slack, her steady breathing a sign that, just as Fabia had pointed out, the child felt safe at last.

Tears bulged in her eyes—tears of love and fear of loss and a heart-clenching tenderness that had her trembling mouth brushing a caress over the baby's warm cheek.

'Don't cry, *signora*...' Fabia bent down beside the chair to place a consoling hand on Sara's arm. 'She is safe now. Signor Nicolas see to it that she remain safe. You need worry no more.'

Yes, she was safe, Sara silently conceded. But she suspected that, far from being over, her worries were only just about to begin.

Alfredo wanted his grandchild. He did not want her mother. He had been very clever in getting them both here with Nicolas's blessing. Was his next move to have Sara removed while the child remained?

Sara knew it was Nicolas from the moment he entered the suite. How she knew she wasn't sure, unless it was a leftover instinct from the last time she had lived here when sheer self-preservation had taught her to pinpoint him wherever he was in this many-levelled villa.

Three years ago he had felt like her only ally in a house of enemies. Even the paid staff had treated her with little respect. And, if she was honest about it, she had not known how to deal with them. They'd intimidated her— as most people had intimidated her then. Now it was a different story. Somewhere along the line she had gained a maturity that stopped her seeing everyone as frightening aliens in an alien world.

Like Fabia, for instance. Whether it was Sara's own firm, quiet manner or the fact that the servant was a new addition to the Santino staff since Sara had been here last and therefore had no idea how Sara used to be treated she wasn't sure, but far from being cold and unhelpful Fabia had gone out of her way to make Sara feel more comfortable in a situation she was so obviously not comfortable with. She'd allowed no one entry into the suite, insisting on answering each knock at the door and dealing with the caller herself.

'The whole house waited anxiously for good news of your baby, Mrs Santino,' she'd explained. 'Now they want to come and voice their concerns and their pleasure to you. But they can wait,' she'd decided firmly. 'You just be comfortable and enjoy having that warm little body close again. I will deal with the rest.'

And Sara had begun to feel comfortable—to her own surprise.

When Lia had awoken feeling hungry and fractious, it had been Fabia who had helped soothe her with the same quiet manner that Sara had recognised as the one she had used on herself. And when Lia, with the usual resilience that children had by nature, had suddenly become her usual bundle of restless energy Fabia had come with them down to the tiny beach.

The three of them had spent a long, soothing hour down there, taking advantage of the late afternoon sun's cooler rays to simply play without fear of either mother or child burning. They'd paddled in the silk-warm water that gently lapped the sand-skirted shore, and built a sandcastle together then decorated it with pebbles from farther up the beach, Lia paddling to and fro with a happy contentment that twisted her mother's heart.

She had been so close—so close to never seeing her baby like this again....

They'd come back up the long row of steps as a threesome, at first with the little girl jumping the steps between Sara and Fabia, each small hand tucked into one of theirs, and later, when she'd run out of steam, straddling her mother's hips, with her tired head on

Sara's shoulder, while Fabia had paced quietly beside them, a kind of soothing quality about her presence.

That had been hours ago, though. Now the sun was setting low in the sky and Lia was fast asleep in the baby's cot which had been erected by Sara's bed. And Fabia had seemingly taken root, Sara thought with a small smile, because she was sitting in a chair beside the sleeping child, quietly stitching her delicate embroidery, quite indifferent to Sara's claims that she did not need to stay any longer.

In the end, Sara had left her to it, coming through here to the sitting room, to flop down on a sofa to watch the sunset, feeling about as drained as an electronic toy without any batteries now that Lia no longer had a claim on her attention.

The last few days, she accepted, were finally catching up with her.

'You look shocking,' was Nicolas's own observation as he arrived at the side of her chair.

'And it makes me feel so much better to hear you say it.'

He sighed at her sarcasm, stepping past her to go and stare at the sunset. 'The child is—calmer now?' he asked after a moment.

'No thanks to you, yes.' For a long while after awakening on her mother's lap, Lia had been frightened, and confused, and—

She sighed, closing her eyes and her mind to all the painful things she could only guess that her poor baby had been feeling over the last few days.

'I apologise if I—frightened the child,' he murmured stiffly. 'But you must understand that I find the situation—difficult.'

'Well, you will no doubt be pleased to know, then, that we will be happy to go back to London just as soon as you give the word.'

'So eager to leave,' he mocked.

'The sooner you transport us back out of here, the sooner the—difficult situation will be over.'

'I wish it could be that simple.'

'It is,' she assured him. 'Just call for your private limousine and your private jet aeroplane—' her voice dripped more sarcasm '—and we will be gone, I promise you.'

He said nothing to that, his attention seemingly fixed on the breathtaking sight of a vermilion sky touching a blue satin sea.

Then he turned and glanced down at her. 'Dinner will be ready in about an hour,' he informed her. 'Do you think you can make an effort and tidy yourself for it? I can understand why you must look so wrung out,' he allowed, 'but do you have to be dressed like a rag doll also?'

The criticism was aimed directly at the way she had her hair scraped untidily back into a pony-tail, and the fact that she was still wearing the same clothes she had travelled in. She looked battle-worn and travel-stained.

He had managed to change his clothes, though, she noted, and was now dressed in a snowy white shirt and black silk trousers. He looked good. Long legs, tight hips, broad shoulders.

'Blame yourself for the way I look,' she threw at him, dropping her gaze from the lean, tight attractiveness that had always been his. 'You may have kindly packed for me this morning, but only the smart couture outfits a man like you would expect a woman to wear. No day clothes,' she explained at his frown. 'Nothing to counter the hot climate, or the fact that I would be dealing with a very energetic, very messy child. And to top that,' she concluded, her voice so dry that you could have scored chalk lines on it, 'you forgot to pack toiletries, underwear or even a hairbrush.'

'That bad, huh?' he grunted. 'I am not used to packing,' he then added as an excuse.

'It showed.' Despite herself, Sara could not hold back a small smile. 'You did a little better for Lia,' she then went on to allow graciously. 'Simply because you must have just emptied each drawer containing her clothes into the suitcase. And— Oh,' she added, 'you remembered Dandy. Now that was really thoughtful. Her whole countenance changed when she saw him again.'

'And what, I wonder, will change yours?'

She went hot, then cold, then began tingling all over as his softly provoking tone sent disturbing little messages to all her senses.

'I will eat my dinner here in the suite if you don't mind,' she said coolly as a way to counteract the disturbance.

'You will eat in the dining room as is the custom in this house,' he ordained. But at least that other, more intimate tone had gone from his voice.

She shook her head. 'I won't leave Lia here alone. She may wake up and be frightened.'

'And Fabia is with her, is she not?'

'Yes.' Sara conceded that point. 'But Fabia is not the child's mother, is she? She's had enough upsets in her little life recently without waking to a strange room and a strange woman and no sign of her mother.'

'The house is equipped with an internal communications system.' He made dry mockery of all her protests. 'One call from Fabia and you can be back down here in seconds.'

'Seconds that can seem like an hour of agony to a child in distress.'

'This is foolish!' He sighed. 'The child is safe! She knows Fabia's face. She knows her mama accepts Fabia as someone she can trust. You have spent the whole afternoon together building that trust! Now you must trust Fabia to do her job without rancour from you, while you—'

'Job?' She picked up on the word with a sharp question.

'Yes.' His eyes glinted down at her, cool and unwavering. 'Fabia has been employed specifically to look after the child.'

She jumped up, a tight band of fear suddenly closing like steel around her chest. 'As a nanny, you mean?'

'Yes...,' he confirmed, but in a way which tightened the band further. She was thinking of Alfredo, wondering how much of his influence was at work here. Had Alfredo employed Fabia? Was she here to wean Lia away from her mother so that the wrench when it came would not be too great for the child?

'I don't need a nanny to help me with Lia,' she stated as firmly as her quaking heart would let her. 'L-look what h-happened the l-last time you employed a nanny! Lia was taken from right beneath her nose!'

'Why are you stammering?' He frowned down at her.

Because I'm frightened, she thought agitatedly. 'Nic, please—' She resorted to begging, her hand going to clutch at his forearm in appeal. 'Don't do this to me! Don't reduce my importance as a mother! I don't need Fabia! I w-won't be here long enough to n-need her!'

'My God,' he breathed, his eyes suddenly dark with shock. 'You are terrified, aren't you?'

So t-terrified that I'm even s-stammering inside my head! she thought wildly. 'L-let me just stay quietly here in this s-suite until you are ready to send us back to London! Please!'

'But what are you frightened of?' He ignored her plea to demand an answer to his question. 'Do you think because the child's abductors were Sicilian that I cannot protect you here?' he suggested when she didn't answer but just stood there staring at him with those huge, frightened eyes and trembling so badly that he felt compelled to lift his hands to her arms to steady her. 'You are wrong, you know,' he murmured reassuringly. 'This place is built like a fortress. Nothing moves outside it without an electronic camera picking it up.'

But it wasn't the outside Sara was worried about. It was the inside. And the people within it.

She took in a deep breath, and tried very hard to grab back some self-control. 'Nic...,'

She stepped closer, her fingers settling tremulously on the centre of his wide chest. It was not a come-on; she was not trying to use female wiles on him here to get him to do what she wanted. She was simply too anxious to know what she was doing or how she was doing it.

'Listen to me . . .' she pleaded. 'I don't want to be here and you don't want us here! If you believe it impossible to protect us in London, then I will change my name—my identity if I have to! Just send us back to England and I shall get right out of your life. I promise you. You won't have to be inconvenienced like this again on our account!'

He stiffened, the big chest expanding on a tense clenching of its muscular flesh. 'You—love this child very much, don't you?'

Why did he keep on asking her that question? 'She is my life!' she choked.

'And the father? Did you love him with the same strength?'

Oh, God. Sara closed her eyes on a shaft of tight pain and wanted to drop her head onto that big chest and weep. Weep. 'Yes,' she breathed.

He stepped away from her, turning back to the window and leaving her standing there trembling with her hands still lifted in front of her where his chest had just been.

'Did he love you?' he enquired after a moment.

She had to swallow to remove the aching lump from her throat. 'I think so, once,' she replied, letting her hands drop empty to her sides.

'Then why did he never claim you both?'

Her sigh held an irony only she would ever understand. 'Because he could never be sure that my baby was his and his pride could not let him accept another man's child.'

'Could she be mine, then?'

Oh, no, she thought wretchedly. Don't ask me that question now. Not when I daren't give you an honest answer!

So instead she avoided it. 'Nic, I need to get away from here. I can't bear this place,' she murmured thickly. 'I never could.'

'Were you so unhappy here?'

Without you here with me? she thought painfully. 'Yes,' she said, and sank down onto the sofa and wished to God that they'd never begun this whole wretched scene.

He didn't say anything to that, and the silence between them throbbed with the heavy pull of her own heartbeat.

Then, quietly, he said, 'You cannot leave.'

Her stomach gave a funny lurch. 'What's that supposed to mean?' she asked warily.

He turned. 'Just what it said. You cannot leave here. The risk is too great. I can guarantee your safety here; I cannot in London.' He gave a small shrug. 'So here is where you and the child must stay.'

'No.' She shook her head vehemently. 'I don't want to.'

'I am not giving you a choice,' he grimly informed her.

It brought her back to her feet. 'Just because you refuse to divorce me does not mean you own me, Nicolas!' she cried. 'I can make my own choices. And I prefer to take my chance in London rather than live under this roof again!'

'You speak as if it were you who was betrayed!' he said derisively in response to that little speech.

'I will not be put through the kind of misery I endured here a second time.'

'Maybe you deserve to be miserable.'

That came straight from the gut, and she squeezed her eyes tight shut while she handled the blow it dealt her.

'But my baby does not,' she managed to parry. 'She is the innocent one in all of this. Punish the mother and you will punish the child. Can you be that callous? That thirsty for revenge?'

'I am not after revenge,' he denied. 'It is a simple case of logistics which decides it for us. This house is easier to guard against a repeat of what you have just been through. Therefore this is where you will live from now on. *Comprende?*'

Oh, she '*comprended*' all right. The lord and master had spoken. End of discussion.

'But I don't have to eat with you,' she countered, throwing herself back onto the sofa with a defiance about her that warned him she was not going to surrender this point to him as well! 'I would rather starve first.'

'And that is being childish,' he derided.

Too true, she agreed. But there was no way she was going to sit at the same table as Alfredo Santino! No way.

'I'm tired,' she said. 'I don't want to dress up and play happy dinner hour with you and your father—can't you even allow me that one concession?'

He sighed, allowing some of his anger to escape with the sound. Then surprisingly he gave in. 'I need to speak to Fabia before I leave you,' he said. 'Then I will have something sent down to you.'

With that, he walked off towards the bedroom, leaving Sara feeling annoyingly, frustratingly let down. Though she didn't know why.

Or refused to look at why.

CHAPTER EIGHT

SARA was squatting by the cultivated border of one of the many white-painted terrace walls, carefully coaxing bougainvillea strands around a wire support that she had just constructed, secure in the knowledge that she could hear Lia's happy voice drifting up to her from where she played on the beach with Fabia, when an electric whirring sound behind her warned her of Alfredo's approach.

She didn't turn, did not so much as reveal she was aware of his presence. But her inner sigh was heavy. In the six days since she had arrived here, she had carefully avoided any contact at all with Alfredo. He came to see Lia each lunchtime, guiding his chair into the suite and staying long enough to share lunch with the baby, and Sara made herself distinctly scarce before he was due to arrive.

It was necessary for them to stay here, Nicolas had said. But necessary to whom? To this man in the wheelchair coming steadily towards her along the terrace? Of course it was.

It certainly wasn't what Nicolas wanted, she thought bleakly, because she hadn't even seen him since the first night she'd arrived here.

He had had his talk with Fabia, their two voices conversing in the quick Sicilian dialect Sara had never quite been able to keep up with even before her Italian had become rusty through lack of use.

When he'd come out of the bedroom again, he hadn't even bothered to wish her goodnight, but had just left.

She hadn't seen him since. The next morning she'd awoken to Fabia arriving with a manservant in tow carrying some heavy suitcases. They'd contained all her personal belongings. Nicolas must have had them flown

107

in overnight from London. A further statement that this was to be a permanent situation. Fabia had also brought a message from Nicholas informing her that he'd had to fly back to New York.

He had been gone for almost a week now, and she refused point-blank to admit—even to herself—that she missed him.

The wheelchair stopped a couple of feet away. Sara felt his eyes on her, sensed him urging her to turn and acknowledge him. When she did not, it was he who broke the tense silence between them.

'The garden has missed your special touch,' he said.

'I have nothing to say to you, Alfredo,' she told him without pausing in what she was doing. 'You are a mean, nasty, selfish old man who doesn't deserve my attention. Or the attention of my daughter, come to that.'

Instead of taking exception to her outright attack on him, she was surprised to hear him give a soft chuckle. 'I would say that constituted saying a lot,' he remarked ruefully.

It made her turn, more out of suspicion than because she had been taken by surprise by his amiable tone. She was quite sure Alfredo could chuckle as pleasantly as that while thrusting a knife between her shoulderblades!

Still, this first real look at him without her being blinded by the horror of seeing her daughter clasped to his chest was a shock.

Dressed in a cream short-sleeved shirt open at the throat and a pair of brown trousers, he was still a remarkably daunting person—remarkable because he had been so drastically diminished in the purely physical sense.

Never anywhere near as tall as his son, he had once made up for his lack of inches with width. Wide shoulders, wide chest, wide hips, short, immovable trunks for legs—all of it solid-packed and tough. But now the width had gone, the muscle waste so dramatic that it had left behind it a mere shadow of what once had been, replacing it with a frailty so obvious that Sara began to understand why Nicolas was so angrily protective of what pathetic amount was left.

The sun was shining down on his silvered head—the hair was not thinning, she noted. At least he had been saved that emasculation. But his skin, though tanned, was sallow and loose, wrinkling his arms and his throat. And there was a lack of strength in the way he sat hunched in his wheelchair, as if the mere act of sitting in it was an effort in itself.

'Goodness me.' She sat back on her heels, too stunned to hold back the next comment. 'You look terrible.'

His answering wry smile was more a fatalistic rueful grimace. 'I hate it,' he admitted, and slapped a thin hand on the wheelchair arm. 'Hate this too.'

I just bet you do, she thought with a moment's soft pity for this man who used to be a giant despite his lack of inches.

Then he was sending her a look that had all hint of compassion draining right out of her. For this man was still dangerous, physically incapacitated or not. Those two bright hunter's gold eyes were burning pinpoints of astuteness and guile, warning her that the sharp brain behind them still functioned at its old breakneck pace.

'You, I see, are more beautiful than ever,' he remarked. 'The child is hewn in your image. Your hair, your face, your inherently sweet and gentle nature.'

'I was a coward, Alfredo,' Sara countered, ignoring the attempted compliment. 'My daughter is not.'

Something she had discovered via listening painfully as Lia had over the last few days let little things slip which suggested that the child had not made it easy for her kidnappers.

'It will be my son's genes which give her courage.' He nodded proudly. 'Or maybe even my own.'

'God help her,' Sara responded, amazed that he wasn't even going to pretend he did not know exactly who Lia's father was. 'If she has much of you in her, Alfredo, then she will need God's help.' She fixed him with a hard and cold look. 'Have you any idea how much you frightened her having her snatched like that?'

'Me?' At last he decided to use his striking ability to fake innocence, actually managing to look shocked by the accusation. 'I did not snatch the *bambina*!' he denied. 'I would not wish to frighten a hair on her beautiful head!'

'Liar.' Blue eyes suddenly hot with anger, she stood up and went to lean over him. 'I saw your expression when you held my baby in your arms! You were glowing with triumph! With everything alive in you, you were staking ownership! Possessive and territorial! I saw it, Alfredo. I saw it!'

It made him gasp, the very fact that she could spit at him like that utterly astounding him. 'You grow brave in the face of a shrivelled old man in a wheelchair,' he murmured feebly.

'Don't try the poor sick old man routine on me,' she said scathingly as she straightened away. 'It just won't work.'

With that, she bent to pick up her coil of garden wire and secateurs and made to leave.

'Don't walk away from me, woman!' he growled.

Oddly, it stopped her. Not the words themselves but the way he had said them. There was a bitter, biting frustration there—frustration with his physical disadvantage.

She turned back to glance at him just as his fist made furious contact with the wheelchair arm, his face a twisted map of angry helplessness.

'I did not take the child!' He scowled mutinously up at her. 'If I had thought of it, I would have!' he added bluntly. 'But I did not!' Then he sighed heavily because the burst of passionate anger had obviously drained his energy.

Sara saw him go a paler shade of sallow, his eyes lose the vibrant spark of life, and her bottom lip twitched in a spasm of unwanted feeling for this man who was her enemy. She didn't know whether to believe him, or even if it really mattered that much now that the deed was done. But she could not afford to relax her guard around Alfredo, she reminded herself grimly. Past experience had taught her that lesson the hardest way anyone could learn a lesson in life.

But nor was it in her nature to be cruel to the afflicted, and Alfredo was certainly afflicted at the moment.

'Are you all right?' she asked stiffly.

'Sì,' he clipped back, but he was leaning heavily on his forearms, his silvered head lowered while he seemed to be concentrating on pacing his breathing.

A child's laughter drifted up from the small beach below, tinkling around both of them and diverting their attention to the sight of Lia dressed in white cotton dungarees and a white cotton mob-cap pulled on over her hair, running as fast as her little legs could take her, away from Fabia who was chasing with a string of wet seaweed dangling from one hand.

Sara laughed too; she couldn't help it. Leaning her thighs against the terrace wall, she folded her arms and watched the chase.

Suddenly the wheelchair was right beside her, Alfredo leaning forward as much as he could to follow what was going on.

'Run, little one. Run!' he encouraged gruffly, a thin hand making a fist which he used to urge the child further.

It was miraculous. In those few short seconds he had doubled in strength, in life, in sheer vitality. And the chase was lost to Sara as she took all of this in.

A tingling on the back of her neck—that sixth sense at work again, probably—made her turn and look up—up the white-walled terraces, to see Nicolas standing several levels above them, his dark face carved in a mask of pained observation.

Pain not for the child but for the father. Her heart squeezed in her breast. He too had seen the change in Alfredo—perhaps even heard the exchange which had preceded it.

His eyes flicked to her and turned cold—as cold as yellow ice. Yes, he had heard, she realised with a small shiver. Not all of it, but enough. He had warned her not to upset his father. Now retribution was due because she had.

'Hah!' said Alfredo, sitting back in his chair with a triumphant laugh. 'Did you see that?' He chuckled delightedly, unaware of the other exchange going on. 'She escaped by ducking right between Fabia's legs!'

Dragging her eyes from Nicolas's, she glanced down at the beach where Fabia was now giving chase in the other direction. When she looked up again, Nicolas was gone.

'Aye, aye, aye...' Alfredo sighed enviyingly. 'To be able to go down there and join in the fun...'

'Alfredo—' Impulsively, Sara knelt down to his level.

'Lia is your grandchild—'

'I know this.' He turned, eyes so incredibly softened by pride and joy that it caught at her throat.

'You love her already.'

'Sì,' he confirmed. 'We—how you English say?— bonded!' he exclaimed. 'From the moment she saw me, Sara! She came into my arms as if she had known them always! I love her,' he sighed. 'She loves me! It is wonderful!'

'She is part of me too, Alfredo,' Sara firmly reminded him.

'It would be difficult to deny this when she is the image of you.' He grinned.

'She needs her mother.'

'Of course!' He looked almost shocked that she should feel the need to tell him that. 'All children need their mother...' he added, his attention drifting back to the beach where the game had now finished and Lia was busy with her bucket and spade while Fabia erected a beach umbrella over her to keep off the sun. 'Nico was entirely devoted to his mama,' he went on softly. 'They would play together—on this same beach—just like that.' 'Rosalia,' Sara prompted softly.

'*Si*.' The gold eyes darkened. 'You named the child after Nico's *mamma*. I thank you.' He gave a small nod of his head. 'It was—kind of you under the circumstances.'

'She was a very special woman, so Nicholas once told me. She—' Sara eyed him carefully. 'She was devoted to both her husband and her son.'

'*Si*.' Again the word held a wealth of tenderness. 'As we were devoted to her,' he added. 'But she took very sick. Then she died. We both grieved for her badly—still do in some quiet moments, though it was a long time ago now.'

'Would Rosalia be proud of you, Alfredo, for denying her son the right to love his own wife and child as she loved you both?'

There was a sudden stillness about him. Sara held her breath, waiting—waiting to see how he was going to respond to that blatant attempt to reach his conscience.

'You presume too much,' he said curtly then.

'Do I?', was all she answered, and stood up, deciding she had said enough for now. She had planted the seed; now it was up to him to decide whether to nurture it or just let it die. But if he did let it die then he would be shaming the memory of his beloved wife. Sara had made that point sink indelibly in. 'Just remember that Lia is my child,' she concluded. 'Try any of your rotten tricks to take her from me and I shall fight you to hell and back.'

His golden eyes flicked sharply to her. 'And how could I possibly do that?' he asked, back to being the man she used to know—the one who could terrify her with a look like that.

But not any more, she informed herself bracingly. 'You know exactly how you can do it,' she countered. 'I am one step ahead of you, Alfredo,' she warned. 'Force me to, and I will use my ace card.'

His eyes were studying her with a gleaming intelligence. 'And what would that ace card be?' he asked silkily.

She didn't have one, but it wouldn't hurt to let him think that she might have. 'If you don't already know then I'm not going to tell you.'

'My son loves his *papà*,' he added slyly.

By that Sara assumed he was wondering if she had some way of proving her innocence and Alfredo's culpability to Nicolas.

'Your son has a right to love his own daughter too,' she responded, and turned away, preparing to leave him alone with that.

But his voice when it came to her made her skin crawl with dismay. 'He has a new woman,' he said. 'Her name is Anastasia and she lives in Taormina. He visits her twice a week when he is here.'

Her eyes closed on the words. And she had a flashback to a week ago when she had lain in his arms and heard Nicolas himself confirm that statement. 'Of course I have tried!' he had spat at her. 'Do you think I like feeling this way about you?'

Cancer. Alfredo was a cancer that lived on the weaknesses of others.

She walked away from him, feeling sick and shaken. When she got back to her suite, Nicolas was there. Her heart sank. He was angry, his lean face stone-like and cold.

Retribution was nigh, she recognised wearily, and with a wry little smile stepped further into the suite. Then stopped dead. 'What's going on?' she asked sharply.

The bedroom door was open, and a couple of maids were busily laying all Sara's clothes out on the bed.

No! she thought on an upsurge of alarm. Alfredo had not already done it, had he? He hadn't—?

'Come with me.'

Catching hold of her hand, Nicolas all but frog-marched her out of that suite and along the hallway to the next, where he threw open the door and propelled her inside. She ended up standing in the middle of a beautiful white and blue sitting room; her eyes drifted

dazedly around her surroundings without taking anything in.

The suite door shut with a controlled click. She spun
back to face him. 'What are they doing with my clothes?'
she demanded shakily.

'Removing them,' he replied. 'The suite was not yours
to begin with. I was allowing you time to settle before
moving you, but, having witnessed the way you could
attack a sick old man, I do not see why I should make
any concessions to you—on anything!'

'The suite was not yours...allowing you time to
settle...' Her mind was too busy sorting through what
he had said to worry much about the angry way he had
said it.

'You mean,' she ventured at last, 'that you're moving
Lia and me up a floor, to the family apartments?'

For some reason her conclusion made him frown in
puzzlement. 'What have you been doing with yourself
this last week?' he demanded. 'You cannot, surely, still
be so ignorant of the changes that have been made here?'

Her answer was a blank look because she hadn't so
much as set foot into the rest of the house since arriving
here. She had eaten all her meals in her own room and
confined all her recreation to the beach and the pool,
which had meant her only having to walk up and down
the outer steps. Other than that she had stayed put, with
no interest in reacquainting herself with a place where
she hadn't felt welcome the first time and was sure that
that welcome would be even smaller this time.

His sigh was impatient. 'This whole house has been
completely redesigned since you were here last—essen-
tially to accommodate my father's less mobile state!' he
explained. 'Oh, he gets around quite freely—as you saw
just now,' he added, with a flash of that anger to remind
her why she had been dragged in here like a naughty
child. 'With the aid of special chair-lifts we have had
fitted alongside the east stairway. But for the sake of
comfort other changes were made.'

'What changes?' she prompted warily when he went grimly silent. She wasn't a fool; she knew Nicolas was angry with her. She also knew, therefore, that he was not telling her all of this for her own health!

'There has been a—reallocation of private facilities. My father now has the full use of what was previously considered the family tier. He needs specialist attention,' he went on. 'Twenty-four-hour nursing. Daily physiotherapy and so on. So rooms on that level have been equipped accordingly.'

'Like a mini-hospital, you mean,' she suggested.

'Yes.'

Alfredo must be very ill to warrant such vast and expensive care and attention in his home, she realised, and flicked a look of pained comprehension at Nicolas for what he must be feeling. His father meant the world to him.

He dismissed the look with a cold lifting of his chin. 'The guest suites, therefore, are now below us, level with the pool, recreation rooms and garden terrace,' he continued. 'Because this—' he made a short, gesturing motion with his hand, which she presumed encompassed this whole tier '—is now my own private wing of the house.'

'Ah, I begin to see,' she said with a small, bitter, wry smile. 'You want Lia and me out of your private rooms and down in the guest suites where we belong.'

'No,' he said silkily. 'You do not see at all!' His eyes narrowed on her face, his next words carefully chosen for maximum impact. 'Your child remains exactly where she is. It is you who are moving. In here. In this suite—with me.'

Silence. She met that with total, woolly-minded silence. He watched and waited, his hooded gaze glinting over her long, bare legs, which had been faintly tinted gold in the days she had spent here already. Her plain pink shorts with their loose pleated style did nothing to camouflage the slender hips beneath them. Nor did the simple crop-waisted vest-top, which gave glimpses of her flat stomach when she moved, hide the fact that she was wearing no bra beneath it. Two firm crests were thrusting gently against the thin cloth in a dusky invitation that he would have had to be totally indifferent to not to feel the hot sting of temptation that hit his loins. He remembered too well how they tasted, how they would respond to the lightest touch from him.

Provocative. That was how she looked. A fine, sleek golden creature of sensual provocation. A woman he would be happy to die inside, so long as those breasts were there for him to suckle while he did so. So long as those long golden legs were wrapped around him. So long as that pink heart-shaped mouth was fastened somewhere on his skin, warm and moistly tasting him as he knew it loved to do.

Not that she was aware of any of this, he acknowledged grimly—not of her own sexual attractiveness or what it did to him.

Unaware. Just as her hands were unaware, he was sure, of the coil of garden wire she was twisting between them, and the secateurs and the fact that her wedding ring gleamed gold on her finger.

His wedding ring. The ring he had placed there. Once a gold ring of love, now a gold ring of betrayal.

Stiffly he turned away from both the temptation and the ring, despising himself—despising her.

His movement set her long golden lashes flickering, blue eyes zooming into focus on his long, tense back.

Then, 'No,' she said in flat-voiced refusal. 'I will stay with Lia.'

He spun back, face fierce, the earlier coldness replaced by something else, something faintly disturbing. 'Are we back to arguing about choices?' he clipped. 'Because you have none,' he informed her brutally. 'You will do exactly as you are told while you are under this roof.'

'Except sleep with you,' she objected.

'You will,' he insisted. 'And you will do it without protest! You owe me that!' he rasped in a bitter rejoinder.

Did he mean by that, that she owed him the use of her body in return for his retrieving her stolen child? she wondered in horror. 'But you hate and despise me! You even hated yourself for what happened the last time we shared a bed!'

'True.' His hard face tightened. 'But if I had wanted the whole world to know that Nicolas Santino was foolish enough to marry a faithless woman,' he threw at her, 'I would have denounced both her and her child three years ago!'

She blanched at the intended insult. He took the reaction as his due.

'As it is,' he continued, 'to the world and this household, we are still very much man and wife. And man and wife share a bed and have a certain amount of marital privacy which does not include a child sleeping in the same room.'

'But you haven't been near me for three years,' she cried. 'How are we supposed to have a proper marriage with three years' separation in the middle?'

Her scornful tone made his golden eyes glint. 'You mean because until now you have preferred to spend your time at our London home where I have visited you on a regular basis?'

'My God,' she gasped as clear understanding of his meaning hit her full in the face. 'You can be as two-faced as your father when it really comes down to it, can't you?'

'We will leave my father out of this, if you please,' he said tersely.

'I wish we could!' she flared. 'But since he lives here too and he knows exactly what state our so-called marriage is in isn't he going to find it rather odd—' if not damned frustrating, if her suspicions about him were correct, she added silently to herself '—that you and I are cohabiting again?'

'He will keep his own counsel,' Nicolas coldly stated. 'For neither does he wish to see his son's pride dragged in the dirt because of this—situation we all find our-selves thrust into.'

'He said that, did he?' she challenged. 'Condoned this frankly—obscene suggestion you are putting to me?'

'It is not a suggestion,' he denied, 'and nor is it ob-scene. You are still my wife in the eyes of the world, and you will maintain good appearances at all costs, Sara,' he warned. 'Or so help me I will let you go, and keep the child!'

Thereby threatening to walk her right into Alfredo's neatly baited trap! she realised, and didn't know whether to scream in frustration or weep in defeat. 'I won't sleep with you, Nicolas,' was what she eventually said, and spun abruptly on her heel.

'Where do you think you are going?' he demanded.

'It's time for Lia's afternoon nap,' she informed him stiffly.

'Fabia will see to the child,' he ordained. 'We have unfinished business to discuss here.'

'Except I prefer to see to Lia myself.'

'And I am telling you you cannot!' he snapped, then made an effort to get a hold of himself. 'This is more important. So leave it,' he clipped. 'The child is as safe with Fabia as she could be with anyone.'

She spun back to stare at him. 'Even her own mother?' she challenged. Then, as a sudden thought struck her, she felt tears of hurt spring into her eyes. 'This is another punishment, isn't it?' she accused him bitterly. 'It's just one more Sicilian vendetta whereby you cruelly separate me from my baby for some nasty reason of your own!'

She had to be crazy speaking to him like that, she realised hectically as he took an angry step towards her. But she held her ground, eyes ablaze, her fingers tight-ening on the coil of wire and secateurs in a way that made his eyes widen in real surprise because it was so obvious that she was ready to use them on him if he gave her reason.

'Put those down,' he instructed.

She shook her head, mouth drawn in at the corners and defiant, like her blue eyes, her whole stance!

'You will not like it if I am forced to take them from you,' he warned darkly.

'I know I won't,' she acknowledged to herself. But for some reason I can't allow myself to cower away from you! Not any more—perhaps never again! she realised with a start, and knew the words would have surprised him if she'd said them out loud.

But maybe she didn't need to say them out loud, she noted breathlessly. Because something altered in his eyes, the anger darkening into something much more dangerous: a taste for the battle—not this mental battle whereby she was daring to defy him, or even the one involving a silly pair of secateurs that he could take from her with ease if he so wanted to, but a far more complicated one which set the tiny muscles deep down in her stomach pulsing, set her heart racing.

'Taking me on, *cara?*' he drawled.

Her fingers twitched. 'I'm not going to let you walk all over me, Nicolas,' she returned. 'Not again. Last time you broke my spirit—'

'You never had a spirit,' he countered deridingly, taking a deliberate step towards her. 'You used to jump ten miles high if anyone so much as frowned at you.'

She had to steal herself not to take a defensive step back. 'Well, not any more,' she said determinedly. 'I am a mother now. And I shall fight you to the end of the earth if I have to but you will not separate me from my baby.'

'This has nothing to do with the baby.' He dismissed that angle, taking yet another carefully gauged step.

Her breasts heaved on a short, tense pull of air, but she held her ground.

'This is about you standing there—' he used his darkened eyes to indicate the defiant pose she had adopted '—daring to take me on...'

Another step. She quivered. He saw it and sent her a taunting smile. 'The coil of wire,' he suggested, 'would make an adequate garotte but would require a lot of physical strength for you to succeed with it. I would throw it to one side if I were you, *amore*,' he advised, 'and concentrate on the scissors instead.'

'Secateurs,' she corrected him tensely.

His mocking half-nod acknowledged the correction. 'Now with those you could do me some damage,' he observed. 'Not much,' he added. 'But some—enough maybe to make this new spirit you talk about feel better.'

'I have no wish to damage you at all!' she shakily denied. 'I just want you to stop trying to bully me all the time!'

'Then put down the weapons,' he urged, 'and we will talk about my—bullying.'

She shook her head in refusal, and the odd thing about it was that she had a feeling he would have been disappointed if she had given in to him. He was enjoying this; she could see the beginnings of amusement gleaming behind the taunt in his eyes.

'Then make your move, *cara*,' he softly advised. 'Or I will undoubtedly make mine...'

Then he did—without any more warning, her half-second hesitation all he allowed her before his hands were suddenly snaking out to capture her two wrists, fingers closing tightly around them then forcing them up and apart until he had her standing there in front of him with her hands made useless; then his body was taking up the last bit of space separating them, chest against wildly palpitating chest, hips against hips, thighs against thighs.

'I like it—the spirit,' he murmured. 'I used to like the soft clinging vine you used to be but I think I may like this more spirited creature a whole lot more.'

'I don't want you to like me,' she mumbled in protest.

'No?' He challenged that. The word challenged it, his eyes challenged it, and the sensual curve of his mouth challenged it. 'I think,' he said very softly, 'you want to be kissed into submission.'

'I do not!' she denied.

But it was too late; his mouth covered hers, covered it and moulded it, moulded it and parted it, and, on parting it, brought every sense that she'd been severely containing bursting into quick, clamouring life.

Her wrists he kept up and level with her head; her fingers were still clenched tightly around her 'weapons', as he'd called them. His big chest moved against her chest, making her breasts swell and tighten. His tight hips pushed knowingly against her hips, and the terrible, wonderful sinking feeling she experienced inside made her groan in denial. A denial he scorned by doing the same thing again. And again. And again—until the groan changed in timbre, gave her away, just as her breasts gave her away, her breathing, the way she sank powerlessly into the kiss.

Then her fingers slowly opened, the two clattered thuds which echoed on the tiles at either side of them announcing the final surrender, and she was tugging her wrists, urgent to free her fingers so that she could slide them into his hair, hold his mouth down on hers, move closer—even closer because her legs had turned to liquid and she needed his support to remain upright.

He let her have her way, set her wrists free so that her hands could find his head while his own hands lowered to clasp her lightly around her slender ribcage just below the trembling swell of her breasts. She gave a sensually unsteady sigh and wound her arms around his neck, moving her body closer to the source of its pleasure, sighed again as his hands began stroking her body, moving downwards until they found her hips where they closed and lifted her against the steadily growing evidence of his own passion.

It went on and on, and the one word which kept repeating itself over and over in her head was beautiful. This was so beautiful. The man, his touch, his kiss. Beautiful.

When he lifted her into his arms she did not protest. When he carried her through to the bedroom she only groaned in protest when his mouth left hers for the moment it took him to settle them both on the bed.

Then his mouth was back on hers and she was lost—lost in the beauty of deep, drugging kisses, of his hands caressing her body as they slowly stripped her of her clothes. She lost herself in the acute pleasure of helping him to remove his own, lost herself in the burning blackness of his eyes as he came over her and into her, slowly this time and deeply; mouth tense, cheeks taut with desire, he made the connection with a sombre need that brought tears to her eyes.

'Don't hate me, Nic,' she whispered.

He didn't answer, his long lashes lowering to cover his eyes, and his mouth came down to cover hers, and there in the full brightness of an afternoon sun he lost them both, lost them in the sheer beauty of a slow, slow climb to fulfilment.

When she awoke what seemed like hours later, but was probably only a few blissfully forgetful minutes, he was gone.

Gone hating her? she wondered. Hating himself?

CHAPTER NINE

And that was it. Sara was trapped. Trapped by necessity. Trapped by her own body, which would respond to the slightest touch from the man who had reawoken it to its pleasures. And did he pleasure her! Night after night, hungrily, devouringly. But she never woke up to him still there beside her, and that trapped her too—trapped her in a tight little world of self-disgust and helplessness because she could not do a single thing to change the status quo, his status quo, where she played the loving wife and he played the ravaging conqueror.

She was trapped by his ruthless determination to appear the master of his own household by making her sleep with him, eat in the dining room with him and his father, where she was polite to Alfredo but that was about all and Alfredo teased her with cleverly chosen words with double meanings that she did not dare react to for fear of bringing Nicolas's wrath down on her head.

And she was trapped by her daughter, who loved it here and, worse than that, adored Alfredo. A daughter whom Nicolas had managed to avoid at every possible opportunity, so they only came together on very rare occasions, when he would be coolly polite and the little girl would be warily cautious. And Sara would feel her heart break a little more each time she witnessed the guarded manner of both.

Then there was that terrible trapped feeling she experienced when twice a week Nicolas would take himself off to Taormina and not come back until late in the night. Those were the only nights he didn't touch her. And that trapped her too, because she wanted him to touch her, she wanted him to come from his mistress and still need

124

her, still need to drown himself in her kisses, her body, her arms, her—

Love.

And, God, but she didn't know how long she could go on bearing all of this—bearing the fact that she did not dare say anything about his precious Anastasia because Alfredo's lies about herself had robbed her of the right!

Then came the big crunch, which she supposed had to do with so much pressure building up inside her. They were a month into this awful situation and Nicolas had not been away once. He worked from his office here in the villa and spent most of his time there, only appearing for the odd working lunch with his father, which Sara was not expected to attend, and every dinner, which she was. And from there he would either escort her back to their room for a night of heated passion or out to his mistress, leaving her to weep alone in their bed. Then her period came, and he added further insult to injury by disappearing to Taormina for the next five nights.

At least she had not become pregnant, she kept on telling herself as a soother for all her other aches. But it didn't help, and her bitter resentment of the whole situation just grew and grew until it decided to explode on the first night he did try to touch her again.

'Get your hands off me!' she spat at him, fighting against his grip as he tried to draw her across the bed towards him. 'If you're desperate for sex, then go to your fancy piece! I don't want you!'

'My what?' He stopped long enough to elbow himself up on the pillow to stare at her. 'Did you say fancy piece?' he asked in amusement.

'You know exactly what I said,' she flashed. 'And you know exactly who I mean as well!'

'I do? This is interesting,' he murmured, using a hand on her shoulder to keep her flat beneath him while he studied her hot, angry face. 'Does she have a name?' he asked. 'This—fancy piece I get my sex from?'

She glared at him and refused to answer. He grinned, his hand neatly fielding her fist when it came up to hit him. 'I can make you tell me,' he murmured. 'You know I can.'

'May you burn in hell, Nicolas Santino!' she spat at him.

'I would much rather burn inside you,' he replied. 'Or her!' she spat. 'It just depends which day of the week it is!'

His eyes widened, cruel mockery riling her on. 'Oh, I see now,' he drawled. 'You've been putting two and two together and coming up with five! That is a very English expression for someone who is totally out of order, is it not?'

'Anastasia!' she hissed up into his arrogantly mocking face. 'The lady this whole house knows you visit twice a week!' she added disgustedly. 'Now get off me!' She tried to push him away but he refused to budge. 'If you want her—have her!' she muttered frustratedly. 'But you won't have me as well!'

Suddenly all amusement was stripped from his voice. 'No?' he disputed softly, slowly, as silkily as a snake's preparation to bite. 'You did.' The biter bit. 'So why shouldn't I?'

She closed her eyes on a wave of helpless agony. 'I can't take much more of this,' she whispered.

'Yes, you can,' he gritted. 'You can take a whole lot more of it. You will take whatever it is I wish to dish out to you, cara! So lie back and think of England if you must,' he derided bitterly. 'But when I want you will provide, and that is not an option!'

No option. He took, she provided. But he took with such devastating sensualism that England, or anything else for that matter, never entered her head.

Afterwards, a long time afterwards, when she presumed he must think she was sleeping, he got up, shrugged on his white towelling robe and stepped over to the terrace window, quietly sliding it open enough to allow him to slip outside. The next moment she saw a flare of light through the fine weave of the full-length silk curtains and realised he'd gone out there to smoke a cheroot. A bad habit she had thought he had managed to kick. He stayed out for ages, and she wondered what he must be thinking about to want to be alone out there like that.

Was he hating himself again, she wondered bleakly for making love to her believing what he did believe? Did he do this every time—wait until he thought she was asleep then slip out there to despise himself in private?

Was it that same self-hate that made him go to the other woman for some kind of succour for his own despised lusts?

'Of course I have tried!' he had spat at her that first time in London. 'Do you think I like feeling this way about you?'

She closed her eyes to try to shut out the hurt that came with remembering the words. She hurt for herself, she hurt for him. And she hurt because of the utter hopelessness the whole situation filled her with.

When she opened her eyes again, it was to the soft sound of him stepping back into the bedroom. Under cover of darkness she watched him go into the bathroom, lay there listening to him running water, sluicing his face maybe, cleaning his teeth.

Ridding himself of the scent and taste of his supposedly adulterous wife.

Then he was back in the bedroom, a long, lean, silently moving thoroughbred who slid back into the bed beside her then lay on his back with an arm bent beneath his head, while between them lay a wide space of white linen emptiness like a huge chasm, with nothing to use to bridge the great yawning gap.

And silence—a silence that was torture.

So the scream that suddenly ripped through that silence shook the very bones in both of them.

'God,' Sara gasped. 'Lia.'

And she was up and off the bed before Nicolas had even had time to react. Snatching up her robe, she began running. By the time the next terrible scream came she was out of the bedroom, hair streaming out behind her as she raced across to the suite's main door. The child's frightened screams filled the air in Sara's throat as she ran to the next door, bursting in to run across that sitting room on legs which were now shaking badly. Entering the bedroom, she found Fabia standing in a hastily drawn on robe with Lia in her arms, the little body stretching and writhing, her screams enough to turn blood to ice.

'What happened?' Sara was across to the baby in seconds, her arms reaching for her, folding her close, her voice murmuring those soft, soothing sounds mothers instinctively murmured, while the little girl's screams changed to aching sobs.

'Bad man came,' the child sobbed. 'Bad man came to take me away!'

White-faced, Sara glanced questioningly at an equally white-faced Fabia who was shaking her head. 'Dream,' she whispered. 'She has them occasionally.'

'You mean—' Sara had to swallow the rise of angry incredulity, force herself to calm her breathing and her voice before daring to go on. 'You mean this has happened before and you haven't told me?'

The other woman looked uncomfortable. 'Not so bad as this,' she said defensively, her gaze drifting over to where Nicolas had appeared in the doorway dressed in hastily pulled on shorts.

The look said more than Sara could cope with. 'Get out,' she said, and anyone who had been present the day Nicolas had cleared the room in London would have recognised the tone. It was chilling.

On a muffled choke, Fabia rushed from the room. Sara turned her back on Nicolas. It was all she could do if she wasn't to react as she was burning to react. 'Shush, darling,' she murmured soothingly to the sobbing baby. 'Mama's here now. Shush…'

'Sara—' His voice sounded thick, hoarse almost.

'Not now,' she said, and dipped her hand into the cot to get the pink teddy, gently pushed it between herself and the baby's sobbing body then began humming softly.

There was a silence behind her—then a different kind of silence. The first was filled with the battle that Nicolas was having with himself at her cold dismissal. The second was the sound of his battle won—or lost; she wasn't sure which—and she knew he had gone.

When eventually Lia drifted back into sleep, Sara did not replace her in her cot but sat down in the chair beside Fabia's rumpled bed and allowed the little girl to spread out on her lap with her warm cheek cushioned on Sara's breast.

She stayed like that for ages. How long she didn't know. It didn't matter. When Nicolas eventually came back, she barely acknowledged him. He went to stand by the window—a habit of his when struggling with something, she'd come to realise. He had pulled on a white towelling robe, and his hands were lost inside the capacious pockets. His hair was ruffled and his profile grim.

'It was I who instructed Fabia not to interrupt us after we had retired because I needed to feel our nights belonged to me.'

Those were, she assumed, the nights he did not devote to Anastasia.

'Fabia is upset,' he continued when it became clear that she was not going to say anything. 'She fears you may dismiss her if I do not make this instruction clear to you.'

'I have no jurisdiction over Fabia's employment,' she reminded him coolly.

'But she does not know that.' He turned. 'She has a genuine affection for the child, Sara. It would be wrong to punish her for something I am at fault for.'

'I have no intention of punishing anyone.'

'Then put the child back in her bed and let Fabia return to her bed,' he urged.

'While I return to yours?'

He deliberately ignored that. 'She sleeps peacefully now. There is little danger of her having another nightmare like that.'

'But I won't know that, will I?' she pointed out. 'So I'll stay here, if you don't mind, and Fabia can find herself another bed for the rest of the night.'

'But I do mind.'

'Do you know what, Nicolas?' Her chin came up, blue eyes as cold as he'd ever seen them. 'I don't really care what you mind about any more. I am staying here, with my baby, so that if she does have another dream like that I am on hand. Her mother.' She thrust that important point home. 'Not just some substitute you decided would do to keep the child quiet while you got what you wanted from me.'

'It isn't like that.' He sighed.

So did Lia, the sound shuddering on the residue of finished tears.

'It's exactly like that,' Sara maintained, soothing the child with a gentle caress along her golden hairline. 'You can barely bring yourself to look at her, never mind take her needs into consideration.'

'Can you really blame me?' he muttered gruffly.

'Yes, actually, I can,' she said. 'Lia isn't the one who offended your pride, Nicolas. I am. Yet it's the baby you punish by depriving her of her mother when she needs her.'

'I was not attempting to deprive her!' he protested, realised his voice had risen and strove to quieten it. 'I was just . . .'

He ran out of words. Sara provided them for him. 'Time-sharing with her.'

He gave another sigh, then surprisingly said heavily, 'Yes. She has you to herself all day. I wanted you to myself at night.'

'Unless I was time-sharing with Anastasia.'

That took him aback. 'You've developed quite a clever tongue in your head,' he observed, 'for one who used to become tongue-tied in any dispute.'

There was no answer to that, so Sara didn't offer one. She had changed, and she would have had to be a fool not to know just how much she had changed. She was no longer the shy, easily intimidated idiot she used to be.

In a weary movement he came to squat down in front of her. His hand came up, gentle in the gesture as he brushed a stray lock of hair away from Sara's cheek. 'Put the child down and come back to bed,' he urged huskily. 'I promise that Fabia will come for you the moment the child shows signs of stirring.'

But she shook her head. 'I can't,' she whispered. 'I can't share that bed with you again.'

'And why not?' he demanded. 'What has changed here that I have not already promised to put right?'

Everything's changed, she thought bleakly. Because I've just woken up to what I'm letting you do to me—again! You're tearing me apart inside—again. You're making me utterly miserable—again.

'What do you want me to do?' he muttered when she didn't answer. 'Deny the other woman's existence? Is that what this is all about?'

It was part of it, she conceded. A big part of it. 'Does she exist?'

There was a moment's silence while his face took on the expression of a man weighing up the odds. Then he got up and turned away from her. 'Yes,' he said. 'She exists.'

'Then there is no point in denying it, is there?' she replied, but his honesty had cut hard and deep.

'You are not going to insist that I stop seeing her?' He seemed faintly puzzled by her calm, quiet attitude.

Sara compounded his surprise by smiling wryly. 'I don't have that right. I am here under sufferance, remember?' She got up, moving carefully so as not to awaken Lia, and gently lowered the child into her cot, aware of his frowning eyes following her and glad that her face was hidden from him by the long fall of her hair because she didn't want him to see what those calmly spoken words cost her.

Then she straightened and turned fully to face him. 'But I do have the right to deny you the free use of my body when you feel the need to use it,' she concluded. 'And if that causes your pride problems then I'm happy to go back to London, take my chances with the bad guys there. But I won't sleep with you again, Nicolas. That part is over.'

He was studying her narrowly. 'It may be interesting to see if your resolve is as strong as your words,' he suggested softly.

Her chin came up, eyes full of a cool blue defiance that she secretly knew wasn't more than skin-deep. 'Why bother,' she challenged him, 'when you can simply go to your—alternative comfort? It is only sex after all, isn't it? And you can get that anywhere.'

His face hardened, all of it—eyes, cheeks, jaw, lips. He knew what she was saying. He knew she was calling his bluff. If he backed down now and admitted he wanted her, not his lover, he would be revealing so much of his real self to her that she knew, just knew his pride couldn't take it.

She was right. 'You know,' he said tightly, 'perhaps I will at that.'

Then he walked out. And why that made her heart break a little more she had no idea when she'd damned well asked for what she'd got!

The next morning, Fabia was all tears and apologies, while Lia was her usual sunny self, with no idea of the trouble she had caused during the night.

It had been a long time before Sara had been able to stir herself enough to straighten Fabia's bed and stretch out on top of it, only to lie wide awake, her thoughts swerving madly from angry defiance at the way she had sent Nicolas off to wretched feelings of despair at her own stupidity in sending him right into the arms of that other woman!

It was mid-morning before she dared creep back into the other suite to shower and get dressed for the day, fairly safe in the knowledge that he would not be there. He was usually ensconced in his office upstairs by now.

So she almost jumped out of her skin when the suite door flew open just as she was coming out of the bedroom, dressed for the day in her usual shorts and T-shirt.

But it was not Nicolas who came sailing in but his father. 'Been sinking your own ships again, I see,' he remarked. 'You do not need any help to ruin a good thing for yourself, do you?' His hunter's eyes pierced her with a sly look. 'You manage so very well on your own!'

'I presume you had something specific you wished to convey in all of that,' she threw back coolly.

'My son has just left for Catania and informed me not to expect him back.'

Gone. She would have sunk down into the nearest chair in despair if Alfredo had not been there to witness the revealing gesture.

'He has taken Anastasia with him,' he added cruelly. 'And suggests you may prefer to return to the other suite. He has grown weary of you already,' he claimed with satisfaction. 'Soon you will be nothing but a spare part around here again that nobody needs.'

'Except for my daughter,' she reminded him, stung, severely stung by his words. 'Where I go she goes; remember that if you're up to your old tricks, Alfredo.'

'Me?' He looked wonderfully innocent. 'I am simply conveying messages. I am happy for you to stay here with the *bambina* for as long as it takes.'

'Takes for what exactly?' Sara enquired carefully.

'For the child to begin to show signs of her Sicilian origins, of course,' he explained. 'She is all you at the moment, I concede that. But it will not remain that way for ever. Children have a way of changing dramatically as they grow. I already see signs of her *nonna* in her.'

His eyes softened. 'The smile, the way she can charm a person senseless.'

All the things Sara had noticed and likened to Nicolas.

'But Nicolas would have to be with her to see them,' she pointed out tartly. 'And since he can barely stand being in the same room as her he isn't likely to see them, is he?'

'Unless I decide to point these things out,' Alfredo said slyly. 'He is already puzzled by my affection for the child. I tell him it is because she was so frightened when she was first brought here. It—endeared us to each other and he accepts that—up to a point. But if I begin dropping little hints here and little hints there he will grow curious and begin looking carefully for himself.'

Sara went cold. 'And are you?' she asked. 'Going to start dropping your little hints?'

He gave one of his shrugs. 'If it looks like he may have had enough of you already, it leaves me with no alternative, does it? I will not allow my little girl to be taken away from me now I have her!' he stated with fierce possessiveness. 'The *bambina* will stay here—by whatever means it takes for me to keep her here! And if that means I have to convince my son to keep the child when he lets you go then so be it!'

The cold-hearted ruthlessness of the man appalled her.

'Or you could tell Nicolas the truth,' she offered pleadingly as an alternative, 'and guarantee Lia's place here in this house!'

'At the expense of my own?' He dismissed that idea with a shake of his silvered head. 'He would never forgive me. I love the *bambina* but I love my son also. I can do without neither.'

'And what Alfredo wants Alfredo gets,' Sara bitterly observed. 'Don't you care how many other lives you are hurting with all your nasty ways?'

'I am sick.' He defended his selfish behaviour. 'I have not got long on this earth. I want peace and contentment in my latter days, not trouble and disharmony.'

'What you actually are is a nasty, devious old man!' she threw back harshly.

'I know!' He actually laughed! His sallow face broke into an unholy grin that made Sara gasp. 'It does my sick old heart good to know I have not lost my brain cells along with everything else!'

The days dragged without Nicolas around to break up the tedium with long nights of passion and—just being with him.

God, she missed just being with him.

And she discovered another thing about herself that rather surprised her. Having made her big stand against him and actually won, she did not have her things moved out of his bedroom. She did not sleep in the bed—at least she saved herself from that lowering indignity. She slept in the bed next to Lia while Fabia found a bed elsewhere. But she knew that her main reason for not moving her things out of his room was that, despite the fact that he did not mind humiliating her with his open liaison with that other woman, she could not bring herself to humiliate his pride by having everyone know she was no longer prepared to live with him as his wife.

And that all revolved around the guilt she still harboured over her so-called affair with Jason Castell. It didn't seem to matter that she'd never had the affair! Nicolas believed she had. She'd hurt him and therefore she felt guilty.

It was crazy, it was stupid, but she could not do a single thing about it. She felt that she owed him somehow. She owed him his pride and he could have it for now. The time to decide what her next move would be would come when he decided to come home.

That happened a week later.

It was late afternoon and she was down on the small beach with Lia. Between them they had just constructed a rather imaginative sandcastle made up of a series of higgledy-piggledy towers moulded in Lia's red plastic bucket, which the little girl had helped fill and then energetically patted out with the back of her spade.

Kneeling there on the beach, with bare feet, legs, hands and arms liberally peppered with fine, grainy sand, something made Sara glance up—that sixth sense at work again—to see him coming slowly down the steps towards them.

And her heart flipped over with a mixture of desperately suppressed joy and a worse feeling of anxiety. He must have only just arrived back because he hadn't even changed out of his clothes. The jacket and tie were missing, but the mid-grey silk of his trousers and the bright white of his long-sleeved shirt said business.

So did his expression, and it was that which filled her with sudden anxiety. He looked like a man on a mission. A man who had made a decision and was determined to see it through.

'The man coming,' Lia murmured warily.

'I can see,' Sara said as lightly as she could in the circumstances. But it hurt to hear that wary tone in her daughter's voice, just as it hurt to know that although they had been here for over six weeks now Lia still referred to Nicolas as 'the man', as she would a stranger. 'Here,' she murmured to divert the child. 'This one is ready.' Carefully she upturned the bucket full of sand. 'You can pat it out now.'

Lia came to squat down next to her, spade in hand, eyes still on Nicolas. He had reached the final set of steps now, the longest stretch of all, made up of five sets of five cut into sheer rock, which took him into half-shadow before he reached the beach itself.

'Pat, Lia,' Sara prompted quietly.

The little girl turned her head and began to pat, but with less gusto. Nicolas's arrival had taken the fun out of the game.

The crunch of leather on pebbles. Sara gritted her teeth and pretended to concentrate on holding the red plastic bucket upright for the little girl to pat loose.

What did it mean? Was this the beginning of the end? Was she about to be banished back to London again?

As she'd requested, she reminded herself severely.

'Sara,' he said quietly, 'I need to talk to you.'

And she began to break up inside, bits of her flaking and crumbling away like some of the badly constructed sandcastles in front of her.

'Of course.' She sat back on her heels and managed to send him a fleeting smile, her eyes not quite clashing with his.

It didn't matter because he wasn't looking at her either. He was glancing grimly around him, searching for something. Then, with a slight gesture of one hand, he murmured, 'Could we...?' and indicated one of the white plastic sets of tables and chairs kept down here on the beach.

'Sure,' she agreed amiably—for the wary little girl's sake more than anything, but also because she was determined to keep her own steadily deteriorating emotions hidden away.

She straightened, making a play of brushing sand grains from her hands and knees with fingers which decidedly shook. He nodded briefly and moved away.

'Me come,' Lia whispered, and took hold of a fistful of her mother's shorts just to make sure she didn't get left behind.

At least it brought a smile to Sara's tense lips. 'Of course you can come,' she assured the uncertain little face staring up at her.

If Nicolas wanted this talk in private he should have waited for a better opportunity. This was daytime, she reminded herself, Lia's time, according to his rules.

'But if you would rather build another castle I shall only be sitting over there.' She pointed to where Nicolas was now standing by the table.

The little girl took a few moments to consider that option, her big eyes cautiously gauging the distance between the sandcastle and the table. Then, 'OK,' she decided, and bent back to her bucket to begin filling it with fresh sand again.

With that, Sara carefully armoured herself, tried her best to still her racing heart, lifted her chin and walked across the few yards to where Nicolas waited.

He politely held out a chair for her; Sara took it with a muted, 'Thanks,' then waited while he settled himself into the one beside her.

'I have a proposition I want to put to you,' he informed her.

The flaking process inside her took on a new impetus. She kept her eyes fixed firmly on Lia and so, she sensed, did he. 'Go ahead,' she invited smoothly.

'I want us to try again,' he said. 'At our marriage.'

CHAPTER TEN

THE impact that shock announcement had on Sara resulted in a complete collapse of everything inside her—just for a moment, but it showed—showed in the way her body gave an ungainly jerk, in the way her breath was sucked sharply into her lungs.

'Hear me out before you say anything,' Nicolas added quickly, obviously reading her reaction as a negative one. 'I have spent this last week trying to find some solution to this—situation we have created between us. There isn't one,' he announced heavily. 'Not one where we both keep what bit of our pride that is left, anyway.'

He turned his head to look at her, while Sara kept her glazed eyes fixed on a point somewhere between Lia and the table. 'I still want you,' he said huskily. 'I find I cannot let you go a second time. So I am prepared to wipe the slate clean and give us a new beginning. I am asking you to do the same thing.'

She couldn't breathe, couldn't swallow, couldn't even think, he had stunned her so badly with all of this. In all the time she had known Nicolas, she had never known him beg for anything, yet that was exactly what this amounted to. He was begging her to give them a second chance.

Tears clogged her throat. Tears for him, because this had to be badly hurting that pride he had mentioned. He had done nothing wrong—except believed what cruel rumour and his own eyes had told him. Yet he still wanted her—despite that. Was willing to try again—despite that.

'Lia?' she whispered thickly. 'What about Lia? She is a part of me, Nicolas. To want me, you have to also want her.'

His gaze flicked over to where the little girl was playing, and Sara's heart wrenched because she knew what he saw when he looked at her.

'I am not a bad man, Sara,' he murmured grimly after a moment. 'I have no interest in taking my own hurts out on a child.'

Maybe not, she conceded—not consciously anyway. But subconsciously? 'Nicolas, you can't even bring yourself to say her name!' she choked.

'My mother's name,' he clipped. 'I find it difficult to—' He stopped, then made a sudden move with his head that had the tears rushing from her throat to her eyes because it had been a gesture of pain, a gesture of raw pain. 'Why did you do that?' he demanded harshly suddenly. 'Why name her after my mother when—'

Because she's your daughter! she wanted to shout, but couldn't because Alfredo had denied her the right.

But her silence condemned her even more in his eyes, and he got up, hands tense, long fingers flexing at his sides. 'I will adopt her,' he said after a moment. 'Then she will legally be mine.'

Oh, God. Sara closed her eyes on a wave of despair. It wasn't enough. It could never be enough! He deserved better; Lia deserved better. She had no hope of ever proving her own innocence but she had to at least try to prove Lia's!

'I am prepared to let you have a blood test taken,' she said huskily, 'if it helps you to accept her more as your own. We can at least do that.'

He turned to look at her, 'Is that your way of saying that you agree to us trying at our marriage again?'

Was it? She pushed her two hands between her warm, sandy thighs and asked herself the same question. Could they build a new marriage when he would be constantly suspecting her of cheating on him? Could she bear it, knowing that every time they had an argument he could throw the past back up in her face? As he had done the last time they'd been together, she remembered. While she had been throwing his other woman at him.

'The past is in the past, Nicolas,' she murmured eventually. 'You have to promise to bury it there if we are to stand any chance at all.'

He nodded. 'I had already accepted that before I came to you.'

Another admission. Another climb-down. Sara sucked in a deep breath. 'Anastasia,' she breathed out heavily.

He grimaced. 'Out of the picture.'

Out of the picture. Did that mean right out of the picture or only out of the picture as far as she was concerned?

'Then—' No. Angrily she bit back that jealous thought. If she could not trust his word then what right had she to demand that he trust hers?

'Your father,' she prompted next, and waited for the expected slap-down for bringing him into this.

But it didn't come. 'I cannot lie and say he will be—happy with the situation,' he acknowledged. 'But he has developed a real attachment to the ch—' He stopped himself. Sara held her breath. 'Lia . . .' The name left his lips awkwardly, but at least it left his lips. She allowed herself to breathe again. 'Perhaps he sees something in her that I do not,' he then added, his eyes narrowed thoughtfully on the quietly playing little girl.

'Has he said so?' Sara asked warily.

His shrug was half an answer. 'Intimated,' he qualified.

So Alfredo had already carried out his threat last week, she noted, and couldn't stop herself from giving a small shudder. The man was incorrigible when it came to getting what he wanted.

The only difference here being that he had not gambled on Nicolas still wanting her.

'It will be enough for him, I think, to know she will remain a permanent part of his life,' he went on.

As if the little girl sensed his scrutiny, she glanced up, her big eyes clashing cautiously with his. It had the most heart-crushing effect on the mother to watch father and child warily weighing each other up in this way.

'Nic—' Her instinct was to beg him not to hurt the child by cutting her dead. But it seemed Lia didn't need her mother's protection, because she straightened up from her squatting position and, still holding that look, began walking slowly towards him.

The air was suddenly thick—so thick that Sara had a suspicion that none of them could breathe it. Lia stopped in front of Nicolas, sent a swift glance at her mother for reassurance, then slowly lifted one hand towards him and opened it.

It was nothing but a pebble, a small, insignificant little pebble. But in terms of importance it was as precious as a diamond. It was a gesture—of friendship. And, more than that, it was a test of his determination to make this proposition he had put to Sara work.

He knew all of that, of course. It was written in the fierce control he was exerting on his expression as he lowered himself to his haunches. 'Is this for me?' he asked gruffly.

Lia nodded gravely. Sara lost sight of them both as a film of moisture washed across her eyes.

'Then—thank you,' he murmured, and took the pebble. 'I shall treasure it, always.'

'Grandpa got one just like it,' the little girl informed him. 'He keeps it under his pillow at night.'

'He does?' Nicolas said a trifle curiously. 'What for?'

'To keep devils away,' Lia solemnly announced. 'No bad men come get Lia if Grandpa keep the pebble under his pillow.'

'Dio,' Nicolas muttered hoarsely, while Sara sat stunned into stillness. Alfredo had done that? Allayed all the child's fears as neatly and as sensitively as that? She had wondered why the nightmares had not recurred. She had thought it was because Lia had her mama sleeping beside her. But now she had to wonder if it wasn't Alfredo's doing.

A point in the old man's favour? The only one if it was.

'Will you keep this one under your pillow? Keep bad men away?' Lia then asked Nicolas.

He was having difficulty answering; Sara could see his throat working. Lia's grave little revelation had managed to reach into him and touch something raw, as much perhaps as it had her.

'If you think it will help, I will do so.' He grimly accepted the duty. Then, as if he couldn't help himself, he reached out to cup the baby cheek gently with his hand. 'No one will hurt you here,' he murmured huskily. 'I promise you.'

She nodded her head in complete acceptance of that promise. Then, with a typical childlike change of mood, she turned and trotted back to her sandcastles.

'Did you know about this?' Nicolas asked as he slowly straightened.

'About your father and the pebble? No,' Sara breathed. 'I must remember to thank him...'

'Don't cry,' he muttered, seeing the evidence of tears on her cheeks. 'She is safe here. You know she is safe! That period in her young life is over. The memory of it will fade altogether in time.'

I'm not crying out of fear for Lia, she thought achingly. I'm crying for you. You may not know it, but you've just taken the most important step in your life—bridged a link with your daughter.

'What will you do with the pebble?' she asked him, wiping her fingertips over her damp cheeks.

'As I was instructed, of course,' he said, pushing the pebble into his pocket then coming to sit down again. 'She may insist on checking,' he added wryly. 'So under my pillow it must go.'

'Thank you,' Sara said softly.

His golden gaze caught hold of hers for the first time since he had arrived here. 'For what?' he asked gruffly.

'For being so—sensitive to her feelings.'

His eyes darkened. 'I meant what I said about trying again.' It was a rebuke, and a further statement of intent. 'What I have not heard as yet is what you want.'

Well, what did she want? Could she live with him? Could she live without him? Like him, she had accepted days ago that to leave him a second time was going to hurt ten times more than the first time, and that had been bad enough. But staying could hurt too if things between them didn't improve. And what then? More pain, more heartache, with the added agony of being thoroughly trapped because by the time they discovered they'd made a mistake he would have bonded with his daughter, giving Alfredo the weapons he needed to win.

'I have conditions,' she said doubtfully.

His eyes did not so much as flicker. 'Name them.'

Just like that. She dragged her gaze away from his and sucked in a tight lungful of air. 'I need to know that you are going to be here for me, giving me your support, whether or not you believe I am right.' She glanced back at him. 'With your father.' She spelled it out carefully. 'With your servants. With any decisions I decide to make about Lia. I want your promise that you'll be on my side.'

Something flickered in those golden depths at last. 'You did not have this support the last time?'

'No.'

The flicker became a glimmer of wry comprehension. 'How bad a husband was I?' he then enquired, very drily.

'Not a bad husband exactly,' she said. 'Just a—busy one.' That seemed to explain it best. 'I've changed since then,' she felt obliged to add. 'Grown up at last, perhaps. Whatever, I can fight my own battles to a certain extent. But not without your added support.' She sent him a wry smile. 'You are the linchpin of this household, in case you don't know it,' she informed him. 'What happens here happens because you want it to happen.'

'I want you as my wife,' he murmured softly. 'My proper wife.'

That sent a flood of warmth rushing through her. 'And I want the same thing . . .' She had wanted to say that she'd never wanted to be anything else, but that brought up the past, and this was the future they were discussing. A new future.

'But?' he prompted.

But don't look at me like that while I'm trying to be practical, she thought, and blushed, having to turn her eyes away from him. 'Th-this house,' she said. 'B-beautiful though it is, the w-way it is designed does not m-make it ideal for creating a relaxed h-home environment for a family. I accept that, things being the way they are with your f-father, we have to live here but…'

His hand came up, a finger gently tracing the heat in her burning cheek. 'But…?' he prompted again, very softly.

'But I w-want my own space,' she told him warily. 'I w-want a kitchen of my own where I can cook the odd meal if I feel so inclined. I w-want a dining room and a sitting room and bedrooms that d-don't feel like hotel rooms, and—'

She stopped, having to swallow when the caressing finger slid beneath her chin and hooked it to make her turn and look at him. His eyes were dark, lazy with awareness. 'You can have it,' he said. 'You can have it all. Commandeer the recreational-cum-guest level. Alter it to your own specification. We will move down to it when it is ready. Anything else?'

Oh, God, yes, she thought achingly. I want you to love me. I want you to pick me up in your arms and carry me up all of those steps and throw me onto the nearest bed and love me! It was awful—so wanton that she had closed her eyes to hide the dreadful yearning. But the colour in her cheeks deepened, making her wish she could die when he emitted a husky chuckle at the sight of it.

'I did not think I would ever see you blush like this again,' he teased softly. 'What can you be thinking, *cara*?'

'It—it's time for Lia's tea,' she mumbled, and hastily got up.

So did he, lazily, smilingly; he came to stand behind her, his hands coming to rest lightly on her waist. 'That was not what you were thinking,' he taunted. 'You were thinking of me in bed, hopefully naked, with you straddled across me murmuring all those *beautiful* words you can say to send this man crazy.'

His hand moved up to squeeze gently that area of her ribcage where her heart was palpitating madly. 'And you know what I want?' he added, his chin resting on her shoulder so that he could murmur huskily in her ear. 'I want to see you smile at me again like you used to. As if I were the very joy that kept you alive.'

'Oh, Nic!' Instead of a smile, he received a muffled choke as she turned and threw her arms around him.

'Y-you were—y-you are!'

'Then why are you stammering?' he demanded. 'You only stammer when frightened of something.'

'I'm frightened I am making the biggest mistake of my life here, agreeing to this,' she thought anxiously. But, for him, she found that smile he'd requested. 'Or something else,' she suggested provocatively.

He muttered something, took hold of her chin, angled it to his own satisfaction then covered her mouth with his own hungry one.

Above them—way above them on one of the upper terraces—a silvered head viewed the whole situation from his bird's-eye position. His eyes were narrowed, shrewd, calculating. As they broke apart, he rolled away from the wall, as silent an observer as the umpteen security cameras positioned around the whole area.

'Let's go,' Nic muttered, turning Sara towards the steps.

'Nic, y-you've forgotten something . . .'

'Hmm?' He was totally nonplussed. 'I know what I want. I am absolutely sure I know what you want. What else is there?'

'Lia,' she said huskily.

He stopped, flexed his shoulders, looked down at his feet and sighed, and by then every bit of Sara's anxiety was back on show. He glanced at her from beneath his sweeping lashes, saw the anxiousness, sighed again. 'Mistake number one,' he muttered, then sliced her a look. 'OK!' he said defensively. 'I will learn, I will learn!'

Sara slewed her gaze away, not sure if he was cross or ashamed of himself. 'L-Lia,' she called shakily. The little girl glanced up, looking like Cupid bathed in a pool of golden sunshine. 'It's t-time to go back up n-now.'

'Don't stammer,' Nicolas said roughly.

'I'm s-sorry,' she choked.

'And if you start crying again I shall not be responsible for myself.'

She bit down hard on her quivering bottom lip. Lia got up, collected her bucket and spade and came towards them, big blue eyes wary because she could sense the odd atmosphere.

'Sh-shall we leave those by the bottom step for tom-morrow?' Sara suggested, doing very well at controlling the stammer.

The little girl nodded, and dutifully trotted off to place the bucket and spade where she usually left them. Then she turned, eyeing both of them warily. 'Man come too?' she asked.

Sara closed her eyes in despair because they hadn't even left the beach yet and already the problems were falling over each other to make themselves known.

'What now?' Nicolas demanded gruffly.

'She can't keep calling you that,' she sighed. 'Not if...'

'You are right,' he agreed. 'She can't'. And with a grim resolve about him that she hoped wouldn't send her daughter running for cover he walked over to Lia, squatted down to her level and said quite coolly, 'I am your papa. You know, as Grandpa is grandpa?'

The little girl frowned and pouted then gave an uncertain nod of her golden head.

'Then say it,' Nicolas instructed. 'Say Papa.'

'Pa-pa?' Lia repeated cautiously.

'Good.' He nodded and straightened and turned back to Sara. 'If she develops your stammer as well as all your other little foibles, she will be hell to every man who comes into contact with her when she grows up.'

'W-was that a compliment or a criticism?' she enquired uncertainly.

'Both,' he said, then grinned at something only he understood. 'Most definitely both. Let's go.' He offered a hand to Sara.

'I hold Mama's hand,' Lia informed him frowningly.

'Ah.' Another small lesson—in rights of possession.

'Your mama has two hands. We could have one each,' Nicolas suggested almost sarcastically.

'No!' the child protested. 'Lia want to jump!'

Sara couldn't help it—she giggled. He didn't see it, didn't recognise it, but it was his own stubborn nature he was contending with here.

'She means she needs your hand as well as mine to jump up the steps.' Still smiling, Sara came to his rescue. 'Which therefore means you cannot hold my hand as well.'

So Lia jumped. All the way up the steps to the first terrace, one small hand in Sara's, the other in Nicolas's. No one spoke; there seemed to be such an agonising poignancy in the procedure that it did not allow for mere words. But Sara couldn't stop herself from glancing at him warily, not sure if he was as relaxed about all of this as he seemed to be. It was such a novel situation for him, never mind the fact that this was his daughter he was indulging. He was a man who was not around children very much. Nor one you would expect to see helping a little girl jump twenty-five or so stone steps.

At the top, Sara turned and held out her arms. 'I'll carry you now, shall I?' she offered. It was the usual place where Lia tired of jumping.

'Man carry me.'

Sara winced, at two things—'man' and the request for him to carry her. It was one thing Nicolas making an effort with the child, but too much too soon could send *him* screaming for cover.

'Papa.' He took the initiative, thank goodness, because Sara found she wasn't capable of doing so. 'Papa can carry you,' he corrected Lia smoothly.

'OK.' The child turned towards him. 'Papa carry me.' And she lifted her arms.

He bent, lifted the little girl on the crook of his arm, sent her a sage look while she stared, big-eyed, back. 'May I also hold Mama's hand now?' he requested sarcastically.

He was trying to make light of the whole situation but Sara could see the tension in his features. He was not finding this as easy as it looked.

The little girl nodded. 'Good,' he said, and reached for Sara's hand. His long fingers closed around hers, and she felt the tension in him there as well.

They moved on, across the pool terrace and towards the next flight. Slowly, almost testingly, Lia slid her arms further around his neck, then slowly, even more slowly, laid her head on his shoulder.

'Don't say a single word,' Nicolas murmured gruffly when Sara could not hold back her thick gasp. 'I am not insensitive to the honour the child does me.'

'I know,' she said softly. 'And—thank you.'

His hand tightened on her hand. But he didn't say anything else. On their own level, Fabia was waiting to take the little girl off for her tea and her bath. Nicolas looked relieved, and Lia didn't protest. Sara sensed that she too had had enough of him to be going on with.

As the other two disappeared, he turned a rueful expression on Sara. 'Do I have you to myself for a while now?' he asked. 'Or does tea and bathtime take precedence?'

Normally it would do, but not today. Today he was more important. This tenuous relationship they had decided to try and build was more important.

'I'm all yours,' she smiled.

It was all he needed. The grip on her hand tightened, and the carefully controlled learner father was gone, to be replaced by the sexually very hungry predator male.

What followed was what she supposed could be called a period of adjustment, where they both tried hard to make this new beginning work for them. They were quite successful at it too—aided and abetted by the fact that Alfredo left the house only a few days after Nicolas had returned. He had been booked into an exclusive clinic in Switzerland, where he was to undergo some valve-replacement surgery.

'Is it dangerous?' she'd asked Nicolas when he'd told her about the operation.

He'd grimaced. 'It may help to ease his next few months,' was all he'd said, forcing her to acknowledge just how very ill Alfredo was.

'Are you going to stay with him?'

'No.' He'd smiled at the very idea. 'His pride would not allow me such liberties.'

That great Santino pride; she'd mocked it silently, grimly.

So Alfredo had gone off with his entourage of medical support and had seemed quite taken aback when impulsively Sara had bent down to brush a kiss across his leathery cheek when he'd come to bid Lia farewell.

'I'm coming back!' he'd snapped, sending her one of his aggressive looks. 'So don't go hoping you are seeing the last of me while you bewitch my son a second time!'

'You may be a nasty old man,' she'd retaliated, 'but I do not wish you ill, Alfredo!'

'Ah—bah!' he'd grunted, and wheeled himself off to see his granddaughter.

With Alfredo gone, some of the tension had gone with him. She presumed that this was a relaxing within herself, but maybe Alfredo had been using his clever tongue on his son also, because Nicolas too seemed more at ease within the general run of things.

Neither did Nicolas spend any length of time away from home, which must have helped. He divided his time between his office at the house and the one in Catania, and she presumed, simply on account of the fact that she hadn't seen him since they'd left London, that Toni must be running the international side of things for now.

Was this another indication of how important this new try at their marriage was to Nicolas? She hoped so. And he *was* trying. They both were, but he had the bigger adjustment to make because he had to teach himself to accept Lia. The baby helped. She was so easy to accept, especially with her dear grandpa gone; she needed another man to adore and Nicolas was chosen as the one.

He was cautious at first, using the same dry wit he had used with the child from the beginning to offset any real emotional bonding. But it was kindly done and, she suspected, defensive. He was treading very warily around this daughter of his who might not be his daughter.

The odd thing was that though Sara waited for the day when he would come and say he had arranged for a blood test to be carried out he never so much as mentioned it. And it was a long time before she realised just why he never brought the subject up. And by then it was too late anyway.

Sara began her redesigning project on the recreational/guest tier. She made Nicolas listen to what she had decided on, demanded his opinion, and to know his own requirements of this little house within a house that she was earnestly trying to manufacture. She made him walk the new plan with her, became irritated by his determination to find it all more amusing than anything else, and made love with him in the snooker room because that, she had told him, was where their bedroom would be and he decided he wanted to try it out first.

'What do you think?' she asked him as they lay on the hard green baize, naked and damp from their loving, their limbs so languid that neither had the energy to move.

'It may do,' he murmured noncommittally, 'but I think we should try one or two of the other rooms before making a firm decision.'

'Sex maniac,' she rebuked him.

'Sadist,' he countered. 'I will have permanently green-stained knees from this experiment! I do not think I want a snooker table for a bed, *amore*,' he decided gravely. 'So we had better try one of the other rooms.'

It was like that. Everything light-hearted, easy-going—except when they made love, of course. That was far from light-hearted; it was hot and torrid and very, very serious. They made love every time with a passion that was almost urgent. She wasn't sure why, but sometimes, if she let herself think about it, it worried her. It lacked permanency somehow, as if neither of them really believed that this—honeymoon contentment they had created around them could last.

Alfredo's operation was a success and Nicolas took a flying visit over to see him before the old man was transferred to an exclusive nursing home to convalesce for several weeks.

On impulse, Sara sent him a pebble. 'Tell him it's from Lia,' she said awkwardly. 'To keep away the devils. He will accept it better from her.'

'You two must try to mend your differences,' Nicolas commented. 'I need you to at least try.'

'OK.' She smiled brightly up at him, thinking sadly, You're telling the wrong one of us, darling. 'I'll try.'

The building alterations went ahead—and were finished before Alfredo came back home. Sara prepared a special dinner to welcome him and made a point of showing him what they'd done to the place. She showed him where Lia slept in her own little room with Fabia's off to one side and hers and Nicolas's off to the other with connecting doors in between all. She showed him, too, another bedroom, close to the stairway where the chair-lift was fitted. 'For you,' she informed him quietly. 'If you ever feel the need to be closer to Lia.'

'I'm not at death's door yet, you know,' he sniped at her. 'You do not have to make concessions for a dying old man.'

'Then I won't,' she responded. 'Forget I ever mentioned the silly room.' And don't say it's me who isn't trying, she added acidly to herself.

'Ah—bah!' he dismissed her. But he was different since going to Switzerland. Quieter, more introspective. Yet as far as his health was concerned he was much, much stronger. It made her worry that he was up to something. Something that could ruin what she and Nicolas had managed to achieve in their relationship.

Still, a few more weeks went by without anything untoward happening. The weather turned colder. Nicolas became busier, staying away from home occasionally, though not for weeks at a time. Sara began planning a playroom for Lia since she would not be able to play outside for much longer as the weather was turning less clement.

They were beginning to socialise again. Slowly. Nicolas seemed determined to reintroduce her to the old social scene but gradually as though he was trying—trying not to make the same mistakes this time as he had made the last time. And that warmed her, made her respond better towards his friends in an effort to show that she too was trying. Or maybe it was because she was a different person now and found she could cope amongst these bright, sophisticated people without feeling intimidated.

Whatever the reason, she did not feel the need to cling to him like a limpet and she did not get tongue-tied when anyone spoke to her. People were reasonably pleasant towards her—mainly, she presumed, because her new cool composure in their company gave them nothing to mock as her old nervous shyness had.

Also, they were curious. She had been off the scene for three years after all. If they'd heard rumours about her and a certain Englishman, then those rumours had never been substantiated. And her marriage to Nicolas seemed, on the face of it, firm. Which left them to assume that her absence from Sicily had been of her own volition—maybe even a result of the way they had treated her. Which meant, in their minds, that if she was back she was doing it for Nicolas's sake, not her own. And, really, no one with any sense wanted to offend him by offending his wife a second time.

So they tried—she tried. And all in all it wasn't so bad. She even found herself enjoying the company of some, her smile growing more relaxed and friendly the better she got to know them.

'You are beginning to manage them all as subtly as you manage me,' Nicolas murmured to her one evening as they were making their way home. 'You will have them eating out of your beautiful hand soon.'

'I would rather you ate my hand,' she returned softly, placing her hand over his mouth so that he could press a moist kiss to her palm. It was her way of telling him that he was what mattered most to her, not them. They never spoke of the past but sometimes, like this time, it would loom up in the silent background of what they were saying, threatening to ruin what they had managed to achieve.

While they were slowly rebuilding their marriage like this, Alfredo was growing closer and closer to Lia. He was rarely out of her company and had even started taking her out with him on some days—to visit friends with grandchildren of their own. At first Sara spent the whole time the child was out of her sight fretting in case something happened to her, but when nothing did she eventually began to relax.

If Alfredo had been behind Lia's abduction, then she was absolutely certain that the old man would now guard the child with his very life.

They were so close, grandfather and granddaughter. Much closer than Lia and Nicolas had managed to become.

Though they were getting better, she had to allow, smiling to herself when she remembered the couple of occasions when she had been about to leave the bathroom, having left Nicolas lazing in bed, only to pause on the threshold, her breath caught, throat full of aching tears at the sight of Lia sitting cross-legged beside him on the rumpled white bedding, her little face earnest while she told him some baby story of her own while he listened, as earnest as she, his golden gaze almost tender on the baby face.

Or was it yearning, that look?

She could never make up her mind. She saw it often, but could never quite catch its true quality.

But at least it was something deeper than indifference or, worse, the resentment she had feared he might harbour towards Lia.

We are getting there, she told herself bracingly. Maybe we have a chance.

Then disaster struck.

It hit on two fronts and with such devastating effect that none of them emerged unscathed. None of them.

CHAPTER ELEVEN

THEY were at a party. A big one. The mayor of Taormina's annual ball. Even Alfredo had come with them, the three arriving together in his limousine, Sara dressed in an ankle-length matte black dress that slid over her slender figure as only silk could.

Her hair was down—at Nicolas's request—but she had woven two slender braids at her temples then knotted them together at her nape. Her make-up was minimal, cool, like the new manner she had adopted for her social face. And for the first time since coming back to him she was wearing the lovely diamond engagement ring that Nicolas had given her before they'd married, along with the single string of matching diamonds at her throat—again at his request.

'You're so beautiful I could eat you,' he murmured when she walked with him and his father into the main entrance hall.

'My word for you,' she scolded him. 'Stop stealing.' And she kissed him, aware of Alfredo's watching presence.

She wondered what he was thinking, this wily old man who had taken a surprisingly amiable back seat in the affairs of his son since he had returned from Switzerland. No rows with Sara. No sly taunts. No goading. She didn't understand it.

The two men were in their best dinner suits, and Alfredo looked quite handsome now that he had gained back a little bit of his weight and his skin did not look quite so sallow, since the new valves in his heart were allowing a better supply of oxygen through his system.

It was a packed affair. People milling from room to room in one of the resort's top hotels. A private villa once, dating back centuries, it had managed to maintain many of its original features, including some priceless art treasures and antiques.

She lost Nicolas quite early on, but occasionally caught glimpses of Alfredo. He was wisely remaining close to the main foyer where the crush was not quite so oppressive for a man in a wheelchair. The evening wore on. She became tired, perhaps a little bored with the affair, and decided to go and find Nicolas to tell him she would like to leave.

She found him standing just outside one of the French windows that had been thrown open so that people could take the air on the terrace outside.

And how she found him destroyed every bit of poise and serenity that she had managed to build inside herself during the last few weeks.

He was with a woman. A strange woman. A beautiful woman with thick black hair coiled high on her lovely head. She was tall and slender and wore a dress of the most exquisite blue silk. And she was standing with her hands on Nicolas's shoulders while his hands circled her slender waist. They were looking at each other. Just looking, but it was enough. The look spoke volumes.

Anastasia. It had to be. It sliced Sara apart inside.

Then came the ultimate destroyer. Nicolas smiled at her tenderly and gently touched his mouth to hers.

Sara saw no more. She turned, swaying dizzily, and stumbled away, through the crush, through the people, out into the foyer where she stood for a moment staring blankly around her, lost, completely disorientated.

'Sara?' It was Alfredo's questioning voice that pulled her round in his direction. Whatever he saw on her face made him blanch. 'What is the matter?' he asked sharply.

'I don't feel well,' she murmured vaguely. 'I need to go home.'

'I'll get Nicolas.' Alfredo was already clicking his fingers to gain the attention of a passing waiter.

'No!' she choked, then added less frantically, 'I w-would rather go by myself.' But her blue eyes were filled with anguish.

'Of course,' he agreed, but he was frowning, those shrewd eyes of his suspicious of her excuse. The waiter hurried over. 'Get my car round immediately,' Alfredo instructed. The waiter nodded and rushed off. 'Has someone insulted you?' he then demanded brusquely.

Had they? she wondered blankly. Then, 'Yes,' she whispered. She supposed they had.

'Who?'

She didn't answer. He wasn't even sure that she'd heard him. The waiter came back. 'Your car is at the door, Signor Santino,' he told him.

'Good. Thank you.' His eyes were still sharp on Sara. 'You will find my son, please, and tell him his wife is feeling unwell and I have taken her home.'

With another nod the waiter dived into the bustling crowd.

'Sara—' Alfredo manoeuvred the chair close to her side. '—put your hand on my shoulder.'

Without really knowing it she did as she was told. With his face set in grim lines, he set them both moving. At the entrance, his driver stepped forward to take the chair.

'See Mrs Santino inside first,' Alfredo ordered. The driver glanced sharply at her then jumped to take her arm; she slid into the car without making a murmur. By the time Alfredo joined her, his chair neatly stashed away in the capacious boot, she was shivering.

He took her hand and tried rubbing it. 'Now would you like to explain to me what happened in there?' he asked. 'You said someone had insulted you. Who insulted you?'

'Nicolas,' she whispered.

'Nicolas?' he repeated in stark disbelief. 'Nicolas, my son, insulted you?'

'He was with Anastasia,' she explained, then began to laugh. 'That should give you food for enjoyment,

Alfredo! I caught them red-handed kissing on the terrace! Anastasia and Nicolas! Why don't you laugh?'

'Because it is not damned funny,' he muttered.

'No, it isn't,' she agreed, and stopped laughing abruptly.

'Are you sure you saw this?' he asked frowningly. 'Nicolas?' he prompted. 'Not just someone who looks like Nicolas?'

Her blue eyes swivelled onto him and they were no longer unseeing but sharp—sharper than he had ever seen them before. 'Are you accusing me of being blind as well as stupid?' she asked coldly.

'No.' He shook his silvered head. 'But,' he said slowly, 'I think you may have jumped to the wrong conclusion here—'

'Defending him, Alfredo?' she taunted. 'I thought you would be happy for me.'

'No.' He was still frowning. 'To both questions. I am puzzled,' he added. 'You see, Anastasia is—'

'I don't want to hear,' Sara cut in. 'I don't want to hear anything you have to say on the subject.' She turned her head away. 'Let Nicolas do his own explaining,' she added coldly. 'For once, this has nothing to do with you.'

He sighed, sounding at a loss, and leaned back in the seat. The car swept them around the hill and towards home. Sara stared unseeingly out of the window, her emotions on ice. Alfredo frowned at the glass partition between them and the driver and for once kept his own counsel.

Until they reached home, when he said gruffly, 'What are you going to do?'

She turned that cold look on him. 'Kill the bastard,' she said, then smiled. 'A real Sicilian answer, that, is it not?'

Despite himself Alfredo smiled too. 'I would wait until Nicolas has given you his explanation,' he wryly advised. 'Only I do not think you will feel very good about the knife in his chest when you discover this all one big mistake.'

The car door opened, the chauffeur bending to offer her a helping hand. She ignored it. 'That,' she mocked. 'From the man who first told me about that woman?'

He grimaced. 'I am a nasty old man. You know this.'

I say things to hurt people.'

'It hurt,' she confirmed. 'Is hurting. Congratulations, Alfredo, you've done it again.'

With that, she got out of the car.

'Will you wait one moment?' Alfredo rasped in frustration. 'I want to tell you—'

'The *bambina, signora*,' she murmured shakily. 'She is very sick. Come quickly. Fabia frightened. Please, come quick!'

After that, nothing else mattered. Not Nicolas and his other woman, not Alfredo, who was yelling at his driver to get him in his chair, not the housekeeper, who paced worriedly behind Sara as she fled down the levels to her daughter's bedroom, not Fabia, who was white-faced with fright, or Alfredo's private nurse, who was worriedly leaning over the little girl, carefully examining her.

'What is it?' Sara said urgently. 'What's wrong with her?'

But he had already lost her. Lost her because the next disaster was already striking. Maria, the housekeeper, had appeared at the doorway, her face a frightening map of anxious concern.

'Ask your husband to call for his helicopter, Signora Santino,' the nurse instructed her grimly. 'Your baby needs to get to a hospital quick.'

Quick. 'That word played over and over in Sara's head over the next few nightmarish hours. Quick as in *now*! It rang in every brain cell. Quick, call for the helicopter. Quick, warn the hospital in Catania. Quick, Signora Santino, change your dress if you want to *go* with her.

Go with her. She ran to her own room to rip the beautiful black silk sheath from her body. In her haste the necklace came off with it, diamonds sprinkling all over the white-tiled floor around her. She didn't even see them as she dragged on a pair of navy ski pants and a sweatshirt, then was running back to her baby's room.

Alfredo was there, cracking out orders all over the place, throwing his weight around at people who did not listen. The helicopter arrived, sounding deafeningly loud overhead. It landed on the beach—the only place for it. The nurse gathered up Lia in a blanket and ran, with Sara running behind her.

'What the hell—?' Nicolas had arrived too late. The helicopter was already taking off. Perhaps it was fortunate. His wife was in no fit state to be wifely. His father was yelling something, banging the arms of his wheelchair in helpless frustration. Fabia was sobbing quietly in one corner. 'Will someone tell me what the hell is going on?' he bellowed at the top of his voice.

'Meningitis,' his father choked out hoarsely. 'The nurse suspects the baby has meningitis!'

Intensive Care. Lia's little body hot and swollen, an ugly red rash spoiling her beautiful skin. Sara sat beside the cot and just looked on as so many beeps and buzzes played inside her head. A nurse kept a constant watch on everything—the child, the machinery, the white-faced mother.

Hours. She didn't know how many hours. Nicolas appeared like a dark shadow on the fringes of her consciousness. Drawn, white-faced, he stared at the sick baby then swayed, bringing the nurse rushing over to grab his arm.

It steadied him. He swallowed, pulled himself up, gave a small nod to the nurse to say he was all right. She moved away again. His shocked eyes flicked over to where Sara sat. Then his face was working with a million different emotions, all of them lacerated.

It seemed to take all the strength he had in him to make him go and squat down beside her. His hand was trembling as it covered her own icy hands.

He didn't speak. He could not. So he remained like that, covering her cold hands, swallowed on the lump of utter wretchedness that was blocking his throat and watched the child with her, listened to those awful beeps and buzzes with her. At some point he sat in the chair that someone had kindly brought for him and maintained that still silent vigil with her.

Doctors came, looked, listened, checked then went. Nurses, swapping shifts. An intravenous drip fed essential fluids and powerful antibiotics into the baby via a needle in the back of her little hand. She had wires attached to her checking heart patterns, wires checking brain patterns. She wore nothing but a loosely fastened disposable nappy and looked pathetic—dreadfully, heart-rendingly pathetic.

At one point they were gently urged out of the room. Why, nobody said, but it was the first time since she'd arrived that Sara showed any real sign of life. 'What?' she breathed, startled. 'Why?'

'Just for a little while, Mrs Santino—Mr Santino.' The nurse slowly but firmly led them away to a waiting room where she poured them fresh coffee and quietly advised them to drink it.

Sara drank some because Nicolas made her. But he didn't think she was aware of doing it. In the end, and because he couldn't stand it any more, he gently lifted her out of the chair that the nurse had guided her into and wrapped her in his arms.

But she did not hold him back. She felt fine-boned and fragile—too fragile. Was it possible for a body to lose weight because of a shock like this? He didn't know, but she felt different, as if she wasn't really there at all and it was just the shell of her that he held in his arms.

Minutes ticked by—more minutes. She didn't move but he did, pressing occasional kisses to her hairline, the top of her head, his hands gently stroking her long hair, her back, trying to instil some life in her. Something!

'Mr Santino—Mrs Santino? You can come back now.'

All in Italian. Did Sara remember her Italian well enough to understand? Nicolas wondered. They spoke mainly in English. Both of them. It was like a second language to him so he had no problem, but her Italian had never been quite up to a full-blown Sicilian conversation.

She understood, because she leaned away from his embrace.

And at last he seemed to find his voice. 'Sara...' he murmured unsteadily.

But she shook her head. White—her face was so white that he wondered if she had any blood pumping through it. 'Not now, Nic,' she said, gave him a strange little pat on his chest as if to say, Don't take offence, then walked away.

Hours, more hours. At some point, Alfredo appeared by the bed. How he got there nobody seemed to know since only immediate family were supposed to be there. But there he was. He took one look at the sick child and burst into tears.

Nicolas knew it was wrong, unfair even, but the old man's tears irritated him because they meant he had to leave Sara to go and see to him.

'I must talk to you, son,' Alfredo said hoarsely as Nicolas wheeled him away. 'I need to talk to you.'

'Later,' Nicolas nodded and glanced round for his father's nurse. She was waiting by the open waiting-room door. 'Take him home,' he instructed. 'This is no place for him—too distressing.'

'But I need to talk to you, son!'

'Later,' Nicolas said again, and went back to Sara.

Hours, more hours, and the crisis point came and went. It was just a matter of waiting now. Waiting for Lia to wake up so they would know the extent of damage, if any. But at least she was not going to die.

They moved her out of Intensive Care and into a private room next door. From somewhere Nicolas commandeered a small fold-out bed which he placed by the child's bed and gently urged Sara onto.

'It's OK,' he soothed quietly. 'I am here. I will stay by her. If she moves I will wake you but you must get some sleep now.'

Sleep. She nodded in mute acceptance and closed her eyes.

Hours, more hours. Another day, Sara suspected, but wasn't sure if that made it three days or four. Nicolas had gone back to his hotel at last to get some rest. Alfredo had been in the day before but she hadn't seen him today. She wasn't surprised; the poor old man had looked dreadful yesterday, almost as sick as the baby.

'I will never forgive myself for this,' he'd said painfully.

'You?' Sara had glanced at him. 'It isn't your fault Lia is ill, Alfredo.'

'It is.' Tears had filled the guilty old eyes. 'That friend I took her to visit with me last week, up in the mountains? Two more children from the same village have taken ill with the same thing.' He'd swallowed thickly. 'It is me who exposed her to this. I will never forgive myself. It is all my fault.'

Sara had smiled a tired smile at him. 'Even you cannot thwart fate, Alfredo,' she'd said wryly. 'This is fate's fault. Just fate. Don't torture yourself with such foolish ideas.'

But she hadn't convinced him. He had decided to take full blame upon himself and that was that. Poor old man.

Hours, more hours. Then Nicolas turned up.

He looked terrible.

He should have looked better, since he had been back to his hotel for a proper night's rest last night, yet if anything he looked worse for it, grey-faced and tense.

He muttered a muted hello. Didn't quite look at her. Pulled out the chair on the other side of the bed and sat down on it. Looked at Lia. Looked away. Looked at where his hands rested tensely on the bed.

And where it came from Sara didn't know. But it did come. 'You know, don't you?' she said quietly.

He didn't answer. He looked at Lia again, his face hewn from rock—a rock that began to break up, slowly, uncontrollably.

'Nic—don't!' she murmured, reaching across the bed to cover one of his hands. His own turned in hers, gripped tightly until both shook, then his head went down on the bedcovers and he wept.

In all her life she had never seen or heard anything like it. It filled her own eyes with tears and sent her stumbling to her feet and over to the door to close it, her instinct at that moment to save this broken man's pride from curious eyes.

Then she stood, uncertain just what to do next. To go and hold him could well be the worst indignity she could serve him right now. In the end, she went back to her own chair, sat down and reached across the bed to slide her hand back into his.

He accepted that, at least he accepted that, his own turning again, gripping again. And it seemed to give him the strength he needed to find his self-control.

The dreadful sound stopped. Then he was suddenly getting up, swerving his face away so that she couldn't see it. He went to stand by the window and remained there just staring out at nothing for a long, long time.

'H-how is he?' Sara asked eventually. 'Your father, I mean.'

He didn't answer immediately, and she saw his jaw clench as if he was having a struggle with his emotions again. Then, 'Back at the villa, confined to his bed,' he answered. 'The—confession took it out of him.'

She nodded even though he couldn't see the gesture. But she understood now why Alfredo had not been in to see Lia today. And understood also why he had told Nicolas the truth at last. He was trying to redeem himself in the eyes of his Maker. Not Nicolas. Alfredo would already know he could never redeem himself with Nicolas. But for the sin he believed he had committed in exposing Lia to such an illness he needed to redeem himself by exposing a sin he'd committed when he'd plotted to rid his son of his wife. Even if the confession would cost him his son's love.

Poor, tormented old man.

Her fingers sought her daughter's small hand. 'I'm sorry,' she murmured inadequately.

That made him turn. Turn to let her see the ravages that had taken place in his face. 'You say that—to me?' he rasped. '*No, no*.' He gave a jerked shake of his head. '*Mi scusi*. I cannot—' He stopped and swallowed; Sara watched him helplessly work with his throat to make it let him say what he wanted to say. Then he gave up; she saw it happen with a surge of sudden despair, saw he just couldn't take any more of this right now. '*Mi scusi, cara*, but I must leave you for a while.' He was already shifting his stiff body towards the door. 'I will come back soon when—',

My God! she thought. I've got casualties all around me! Lia here in this bed, Alfredo sick with guilt back at the villa, and now Nicolas is going to walk out of here sick with shock and horror and goodness knows what else.

But she could not let him walk out in the state he was in. 'No—Nic!' she protested, jumping up to rush over to him. 'Don't go!' In an effort to get through to him she threw herself against his chest. 'I need you here. *We need you here!*'

'God, yes,' he breathed. 'Of course you do. And once again I was being—' His big chest heaved on the lack of words. His arms came around her, but they didn't mould to her, didn't hold her, not in the usual way. It was as if the shock he was experiencing had locked all his joints up; everything worked stiffly, as if even the simplest gesture was an effort.

'Come and sit down again,' she urged. 'Please…' She began slowly drawing him back to the bed. 'She's been moving a little today…' She managed to get him to sit in her chair. 'Fingers, toes…'

Having got him this far, she was suddenly at a loss to know what to do next. He was obviously in deep shock. When she had been in deep shock he had ruthlessly poured brandy down her throat, she remembered. But she had no brandy. And—

He was staring at Lia. Staring at her with such a wealth of vulnerable love in his eyes that she suddenly realised that the child might well be his shot of brandy.

'I w-won't be long,' she murmured carefully. 'Now you're here I can go and f-freshen up, and maybe get myself a coffee from the machine...'

Outside the door, she wilted like a wet rag against the wall, a trembling hand going up to rub wearily at her aching brow. All of this coming on top of Lia's illness was just about as bad as timing could get.

Now she had Nicolas to worry about, and Alfredo to worry about—and even herself to worry about, because she wasn't sure what all of this was going to mean.

And Anastasia to worry about.

That brought her abruptly away from the wall, a stinging, hot, bitter poison called jealousy pouring into her blood.

When she went back into the room, Nicolas's face had lost that shattered look and he seemed more—composed. He didn't mention his father's confession again. So neither did she. Nor did she mention Anastasia. But both spectres hovered in the background, waiting to swoop on them when the moment was right. The fact that the sick baby was taking priority only delayed the inevitable; it did not remove it.

More hours. Another full day and night when Sara slept on the little bed by her daughter and Nicolas went back to his hotel to sleep.

In the morning he came back, bringing a change of clothes with him for Sara. She took them gratefully and went off to shower and change into the plain jeans and white overshirt.

When she walked back into the room, she stopped dead, her heart squeezing at the sight of Nicolas half sitting at the head of the bed with Lia, tubes and all, cradled across his chest.

'She awoke just a minute ago,' he said. His eyes were glazed with tears. 'She knew me.'

Like the last time the rigid control which stressful situations demanded had deserted her, Sara's legs went from beneath her. Only this time it wasn't Nicolas who caught her before she hit the ground but the doctor hurrying to the alarm call that Nicolas had sent out when the baby had opened her eyes.

More hours. More waiting. Tests, deliberations, during which Nicolas became Sara's constant support and Lia woke fitfully, showing hopeful signs each time that there had been no long-term effects.

Then official confirmation. 'No damage. You got her here soon enough. Another week and you can take her home.'

They arrived back at the villa on a crisp, sunny morning when everything looked brighter, clearer, more acutely defined. Lia was still weak, still slept away most of the hours in the day, but as soon as they walked into the main hallway she lifted her head from Nicolas's shoulder and smiled as if relieved to be back.

'Where's Grandpa?' she said.

Grandpa, who had not been seen by Sara in over a week. Grandpa, whom the child must have missed, though she hadn't said anything. Grandpa. Just hearing the child mention him made Nicolas's face set into a stone-cold mask.

Yet is was Nicolas who replied, 'He is here,' he assured the little girl. 'Eager to see you. If I pass you to Fabia she will take you right to him now, if you like.'

Lia went happily, leaving Sara and Nicolas standing alone in the main hallway, both tense, both aware that the spectre of truth was getting closer.

'Nic—your father...' It was Sara who decided to bring it closer.

And Nicolas who grimly pushed it away again. 'Not now,' he said curtly. 'I have not the time.' He glanced at his watch—not at her. Nicolas had not let his eyes clash with hers for a long time—not since his father had made his grand confession. 'I have to go out,' he informed her coolly. 'To Palermo. Business—I have let it slide during all of this.'

But that wasn't the real reason why he wanted to leave, and Sara knew it. 'When will you be back?' she asked huskily.

'I cannot be sure. A few days.' He sounded impatient, eager to be gone. 'It depends on how much needs my attention—'

'I need your attention!' she bit back angrily.

'*Don't!*'

She blanched at the violence in the rough-voiced command and actually took a nervous step back from him. 'So we don't count any more, is that it?' she said bitterly. 'Crisis over, so you can now turn your attention to other things!'

Like Anastasia and how good she can make you feel! she added silently.

'That is not what I am doing,' he denied heavily. 'I just need some time—my own space while I come to terms with—with—'

'With what?' she challenged. 'With what your father's confession is going to mean to you? Your life? Your own damned lies?'

'Lies?' His golden eyes sharpened, actually focused directly on her questioningly. 'What lies?'

Oh, God, she thought bitterly. He does that as well if not better than his father does! 'Your father—'

'Leave him out of this!' he hissed, going stone-like again.

Sara sucked in a tense breath. 'We are all victims here, in case that point has escaped you,' she said tightly. 'Including your father!' His eyes flashed a warning; she angrily ignored it. 'He was a proud man, who was proud of his son and wanted the very best he could get for him. It struck right at the heart of his pride when you offered him me instead. So he went to war, and became a victim of his own desire to win over me, no matter what. He won the battle, Nicolas,' she said grimly, 'but he lost the war. Because he then had to live with the knowledge that, in alienating you from me, he had also alienated himself from his own grandchild!'

'Which is why I will never forgive him,' he grated. 'I believed in him.' And at last the real truth of it came spilling out. 'I trusted him as I trusted no other person, and he used that against me—deliberately and cynically used my unquestioning trust in him as a weapon against me!'

'Me, Nicolas. Me!' Sara corrected him. 'He used it against me, not you!'

'What's the difference?' he rasped. 'You *were* me! Mine!' It was fiercely possessive. 'He took the only other thing besides himself that I held dear in my life and twisted it into something ugly! *Ah, Dio!*' he choked, his dark head jerking with a wrench of disgust. 'I cannot talk about this. It offends me. It offends you! All I know is that what he did to me I did to you. I took your trust, your belief in me and destroyed it!'

Not with this, you didn't, she thought coldly. You've destroyed me with Anastasia.

'So what are you intending to do?' she asked. 'Punish a dying old man by pretending he doesn't exist in your life—just as you once punished me by pretending I did not exist?'

'I am allowing him to keep the love of his grand-daughter,' he snapped. 'Which is more than he allowed me!' His expression turned hard and bitter. 'Of course,' he then added less passionately, 'you may do as you wish. I will support any decision you make about both my father's rights where the child is concerned—' Lia was back to being 'the child'! she noted angrily '—and my own rights where you are concerned.'

'In other words,' she choked, 'you're giving up on us!'

His big chest moved in a huge intake of air. 'I am giving up on the right to decide,' he amended. 'I have no rights,' he then added gruffly. 'I rescinded them the day I placed my father's word above your word.'

Or are rescinding them to leave you free to go to Anastasia! Sara corrected him silently.

'Then go and do whatever it is you want to do, Nicolas,' she sighed, turning away from him in disgust. 'For I rescind the right to give a damn!'

CHAPTER TWELVE

The infuriating thing about it was that he went! Just walked out of the house without another word!

And from everything seeming so wonderfully fine a couple of weeks ago it now felt as if Sara's whole world had come crashing down at her feet again!

'Alfredo,' she murmured heavily. Again it was Alfredo. Not deliberately this time, but once again he had pulled the linchpin out from under her. Her linchpin—his own linchpin!

It was time, she supposed, to go and see how much damage the old man had done to himself.

As she was making her way to Alfredo's rooms, she met Fabia on her way out with Lia fast asleep in her arms. Sara smiled at the other woman, tousled her daughter's curls and kept going.

Alfredo's nurse opened the door at her knock. She looked faintly relieved that it was her, which made Sara wonder if she had worried it might be Nicolas on the rampage. The nurse was rarely away from Alfredo's side, so it was logical to assume that she could have overheard at least part of the conversation that must have taken place between father and son when Alfredo had made his grand confession.

He was in his sitting room, his wheelchair facing out towards the window, his thin shoulders hunched, silvered head lowered. When he heard her come in, he turned sharply, those hunter's gold eyes looking hunted for a change.

'You foolish, foolish old man,' Sara scolded. 'Why did you do it?'

'I had to do it,' he said thickly. 'I owed it to the *bambina*. You have always been right about me. I am a wicked, wicked old man!'

Now a broken old man, she thought heavily, and went forward, her arms automatically offering comfort where none was expected. And for the second time a Santino male wept in front of her. It was amazing, because she had thought neither of them capable of crying.

'He will never forgive me,' Alfredo declared long minutes later when the weeping had subsided. 'But I can live with that—die with it,' he added bleakly. 'But I could not live with my own wickedness any longer.' He sniffed, and blew his nose on the handkerchief Sara produced. 'I have not been living well with it since I drove you away from here then had to witness what my plotting had done to my son!' he confessed. 'He missed you, Sara! And I had to watch it happen, watch him show the same grief he had shown when his *mamma* died and know that it was by my hand that he was feeling that bad again! By my hand that he was being denied the right to love his own daughter!'

'But you're a clever man, Alfredo!' She sighed impatiently. 'Couldn't you have found some way to put it right without having to admit the truth?'

He nodded. 'I had every intention of trying to put things right,' he informed her. 'I came to London—with the express purpose of coming to see you, to talk to you, maybe...,' he sighed '...beg your help in putting this nasty business right without losing my son. But I took ill.'

Sara stared at him. 'I remember Toni telling me that you took ill in London! You were coming to see me?' she said in surprise.

'Sì.' He nodded. 'Since then... Well—' he slapped the wheelchair '—you see since then. I have been in no fit state to do anything. I can barely take care of myself any more!' He stopped to swallow thickly. 'Then the *bambina* was taken,' he continued gruffly. 'And suddenly I was being given a chance to put things right because Nicolas was having the little one flown directly out here, to me—to my safe-keeping! I could not believe my luck—'

'What?' Sara cut in sharply. 'What did you just say, Alfredo?'

He looked blank for a moment while he thought back over what he had been saying. 'You mean about Nicolas having Lia flown out to Sicily?' His shoulders moved as if he was shrugging off the fact that he was about to let out another secret.

'She was recovered in England,' he informed her. 'Nicolas was very clever,' he added proudly. 'Very cunning. He had the kidnappers tracked via satellite links with their mobile telephones, discovered their hide-out, then played a shrewd game whereby he split the gang up by agreeing to a drop-off place for the money several miles away from where they held Lia. Then a team of special agents went in to snatch back the child while Toni kept the appointment with the money. It was very clever, very slick; Lia never knew a thing about it. Nic had her safely on a plane to come here before she even woke up!'

'But...' Sara was struggling to take all of this in. 'Why did they need special agents to snatch her back if the ransom was...?' Her voice dried up, her whole blood system with it, when the look on Alfredo's face sent the answer shooting into her head. 'Oh, God,' she choked. 'The kidnappers had no intention of giving her back, did they?'

'We will never know that, *cara*,' Alfredo said grimly. 'But, on the evidence of past cases, no. Lia had too small a chance of coming back to you alive so Nicolas had to make the difficult decision to take her back himself. It was not easy for him,' he sighed. 'She was your whole life and to risk hurting her meant him hurting you too. But everyone involved agreed that he had no choice. So...' His shrug said the rest.

'Then he had her flown directly to me.' His expression showed how good that made him feel. 'Ah, it was love at first sight!' he sighed. 'Me and the *bambina* are like—

that. He crossed two bony fingers, but Sara barely noticed because she was still having difficulty taking in all the rest.

'But why did he have her flown out here before I'd even seen her?' she breathed.

The old man looked at her sagely. 'I would have thought that was obvious,' he mocked. 'He had seen you again. Made love to you again. And he could not let you go a second time.'

'You know we—?' She stopped on an embarrassed gasp, a hot blush flooding up her cheeks. 'But how—?'

'Because you just told me.' He grinned, that old devilish look back on show. 'Those pretty cheeks of yours are a dead give-away, *cara*. They always were. But then,' he added drily, 'my son loves you. There was no real chance that he could be with you and stop himself from making love to you.'

'So, what is Anastasia?' she put in cynically. 'An aberration?'

'Anastasia?' He frowned. 'But did you not ask Nicolas about Anastasia?'

Folding her arms, she got up and moved away, going to stand and stare out of the window much as Nicolas did when disturbed about something. 'What was there to ask?' she said dully. 'I know what I saw.'

'As my son knew what he saw when he found you with Castell?' Alfredo prompted slyly.

She turned, blue eyes narrowed. 'Are you trying to suggest that you set that little scene up at the mayor's ball?' she quizzed him.

'No—no!' he denied, then glanced at her and grimaced. 'But I will forgive you for immediately jumping to that conclusion. Why not, after all?' He gave another one of his shrugs. 'I am a wicked old man. I tell lies. Big lies like—my son has a new woman called Anastasia he visits twice a week. To make you jealous—you know—begin seeing him as the big, sexy man you used to see, eh?' he added roguishly.

'Sorry—' Sara shook her head at that one ' —but Nicolas told me about his affair with her, so you aren't going to trick me by pretending it was just one of your meddling lies,' she warned.

'He told you?' Alfredo looked puzzled—then grinned. 'He has his *papá's* cunning, that one. He too decided to make you burn with jealousy—as you had made him burn once over Castell.'

To make her burn with—?

'Oh, I'm not staying here to listen to you twist everything into knots!' Sara sighed impatiently and moved off towards the door. 'You are too darn cunning for your own good, Alfredo!'

'But I make you think, heh?' he called after her goadingly. 'Your natural fair-mindedness will now make you question your right to condemn my son without a hearing.'

Well, did it? she asked herself impatiently for the umpteenth time in as many days. She was walking alone along the shore, as she had taken to doing often over the last few miserable days, even though the weather had turned cold and the skies became overcast.

Long days. Cold, empty days with no Nicolas beside her. None of his quiet, calm strength. None of his warmth in her bed. None of his kisses and mind-blowing caresses that—

And does that kind of thinking help? she asked herself sternly. Just because Lia is getting better by the day, and no longer requires your full attention, it does not mean you have to turn your thoughts in that direction!

But she missed him. And it hurt—actually hurt like a toothache. And she wanted him to come home because, for all his cunning, Alfredo was right—she did not have the right to condemn Nicolas without a fair hearing.

And anyway, did one small kiss on a public terrace even begin to constitute a betrayal?

'Nic,' she whispered achingly to the cold grey sea. 'Oh, Nic…',

It began to rain, quite suddenly—an absolute deluge that completely halted her miserable thoughts and sent her running as fast as she could for cover. By the time she reached the villa steps she was drenched to the skin. She began running upwards, head down to shield her face from the worst of the rain, so she was not aware of the person hurrying down the steps with a big umbrella open ready for her—until she cannoned right into the solid wall of his chest.

She cried out, almost toppling backwards with the impact, and would have done if a hand had not caught her arm to steady her. She looked up, a shaken thank-you ready on her lips, then was struck silent when she found herself staring into a pair of guarded golden eyes.

Nicolas.

Nicolas, who had come home at last while she had been down on the beach. Nicolas, who had thoughtfully snatched up an umbrella to come and shelter her from the rain.

It was Nicolas she had just cannoned into.

Déjà vu.

The sense of having been in this situation once before swept over her in a hot, tingling wave, followed by an ache so wretched that it filled her eyes with tears. Why, she wasn't sure—until the next words left her thickened throat without her even knowing that they were there to be said.

'Drop your wallet again, Nicolas,' she whispered.

He stiffened up like a board, instant comprehension lifting his big chest on a harsh inward drag of air, the eyes changing from guarded gold to a dark, molten bronze that was almost—pained.

He stood there like that, silent, unbreathing—they both did—for what seemed like an age while Sara felt the complete breakdown of her mental processes begin to shatter her insides because this time—this time it was she who was doing the pleading, she who had just lowered her pride and exposed her real feelings to him.

With those impulsively spoken words, it was she who was asking that they try again.

And that pained look in his eyes was telling her she had made a mistake.

Oh, God—she looked down and away—a terrible, terrible mistake.

He breathed out at last, his body shuddering with the effort. Then, 'Come on,' he muttered, his arm reaching out to fold her to him. 'Let's get out of this rain.'

They went up the rest of the steps together, he holding the umbrella over both of them, she huddled to his side, too shaken and horrified at herself to say another word as he guided her straight to their bathroom where he grabbed a towel and pushed it at her.

'Get those wet clothes off,' he said, 'and dry yourself.'

He turned away to go back into the bedroom. By the time he came back carrying her white towelling robe she was shivering inside the big bath towel—not because she was cold but because she was suffering from shock at her own stupid impulsiveness.

She couldn't even look at him. He said nothing, just grimly handed her the bathrobe and waited while she pushed her arms into it; then he silently produced her hairdryer.

But when she went to take it from him he shook his head. 'I'll do it. Throw your hair forward.'

Too appalled at herself to argue, she did as he bid. And in the next moment heated air was being directed onto her long, wet hair.

She said nothing—couldn't. Neither did he. And the tension between them grew thicker and thicker as the minutes ticked by, until, just when she thought she could stand it no longer, the dryer was switched off, and she found herself standing there in the sudden stunning silence surrounding them, holding her breath, trembling from head to toe, head still bent forward so that she could keep her wretched face hidden behind her hair.

Why had she said something as crazy as that? she asked herself painfully. She hadn't meant to say it. She hadn't even *wanted* to say it!

Now she felt a fool—a silly, bumbling fool. But, worse than that, she knew she had shocked him, rendered him so utterly embarrassed by her silly, stupid—

Something landed at her feet. Her eyes, glazed with wretched tears, burned into focus then just stared at the floor as Nicolas turned and walked away.

It was his wallet.

The tears came back, a muffled sob mounting in her throat. She stared at the wallet, stared until the tears blurred it out of focus again, then she was bending to pick up the fine leather, lovingly smoothing it between trembling fingers while she came to terms with what this really meant.

No mistake. And, far from being embarrassed by her silly outburst, Nicolas had understood!

This was their olive branch. Hers to him. His to her. A wonderful, beautiful olive branch!

He was standing by the bed with his back to her when she came out of the bathroom. Head down, shoulders hunched, hands thrust into his trouser pockets.

Her legs were shaking so much that she had to concentrate hard to get them to carry her over to him. 'Excuse me,' she murmured unsteadily, 'but did you drop this?' She held the wallet out towards him.

He turned, hands still in pockets, shoulders still hunched, his chin down, eyes lowered. Then he simply stood there, staring at the black leather wallet—stared at it until her throat grew thick and her fingers began to tremble.

She swallowed, eyes shining with unshed tears. 'Nic?' she prompted huskily, pushing the wallet a little closer.

He looked up, eyes so black that she could see no colour in them at all, just the reflection of her wretched self. 'Do you know what it did to me the first time you stood in front of me like this?' he asked gruffly.

She nodded, mouth quivering. Love-struck, he'd called it then. Utterly love-struck. 'Me too,' she whispered.

He breathed in—no, sucked in air, his whole body shuddering with the effort. 'Well, it was nothing compared to what I am feeling right now. Nothing—you understand?'

Did she? She nodded again, hoping she understood. Oh, hoping she did! 'Take the wallet, Nic. Please,' she begged.

He shook his head. 'I first need your forgiveness.'

What for? For not believing in her? For Anastasia?

'It is what I came back for,' he continued roughly. 'Whatever else you decide to do about us, I need your forgiveness.'

'You have it,' she said, meaning it. He could have anything he wanted so long as he went on looking at her like that. 'Anything,' she told him thickly. 'Just take back the wallet. I need you to take back the wallet!'

He took another of those deep breaths, but let this one out slowly—and at last reached out and took the wallet. Took it and immediately tossed it aside to reach for her instead.

After that, she wasn't sure how it all happened—whether it was his doing or her own—but suddenly her arms were around his neck and her legs were wrapped around his waist, and they were kissing hungrily, urgently, devouring each other as he turned to topple them both onto the bed.

Her robe fell apart, helped, she thought, by his hands, though it was difficult to say because her arms and legs were still wrapped tightly around him as if her very life depended on holding on to him like this.

It was wild, frenzied almost—the kiss, the way his hands moulded and shaped her body, her hair completely surrounding them both, their breathing completely out of control—senses completely out of control!

'Sara...' He managed to drag his lips sideways enough to murmur her name against her cheek. His mouth was warm and moist, and so necessary to her mouth that she chased it. 'Sara...' He tried again, then groaned when she captured him, their lips, tongues fusing. He allowed himself to sink down into the heat of it for another short, greedy moment before he murmured raspingly, 'You have to let go of me, *mi amore*. I cannot hold you properly while you cling like this.'

But her limbs only tightened. 'I can't let go,' she whispered shakily. 'I think I must be in shock because I just can't let go!'

His sigh shook them both as he levered himself up on his elbows, hands trembling when he tried to brush her hair away from their faces. She opened her eyes, found him gazing down at her with those blackened eyes full of grim concern.

'I am going nowhere,' he told her sombrely. 'I promise you. I will never move from this bed if this is where you want me to stay.'

'Always?' It was crazy, a stupid conversation, yet so incredibly important!

'Until the day I die if that is what it will take,' he vowed.

'Take for what?' she whispered.

'For you to feel loved by me again.'

The tears came back to her eyes. 'And do you?'

Pain dragged at his features. 'I never stopped,' he said thickly. 'How could I? You are the other part of me that is missing when I am not with you.' He lowered his mouth and kissed her again, slowly this time, lovingly. 'You feel the need to hold onto me like this,' he murmured. 'But it is I who will never let you go again. Why else do you think I came rushing back here when I heard what you were going to do?'

She frowned. 'Do?'

He nodded, his hand gentle as it smoothed the tears from her cheeks. 'When you put my father into a state of high panic by telling him you were going to leave here,' he explained, 'he called me up, weeping and wailing and yelling at me because you wanted to take his grand-daughter away, and—' He stopped, his eyes suddenly glassing over as comprehension began to hit him.

It had hit Sara several seconds sooner, and if it did nothing else it allowed her to loosen the grip she had on him, her legs and arms slackening, while she concen-trated on biting her kiss-swollen bottom lip to stop herself smiling.

Then, 'My God,' he gritted. 'He was lying to me, wasn't he? The manipulative old devil was putting on a pathetic act to make me jump to his bidding!'

'He assures me he knows he's a wicked old man,' Sara put in soothingly.

'I should kill him,' Nicolas muttered.

'Oh, don't do that!' she cried, looking genuinely alarmed. 'Your daughter will never forgive you! She loves that nasty old man!'

She shouldn't have said that; she realised it the moment the words left her mouth and his face suddenly dar-kened, his body rolling sideways out of her slackened grasp.

'My daughter,' he muttered. 'The child I rejected before she was even born, because of him.'

'Oh, don't,' she murmured, coming to lean over him, arms holding now instead of clinging. 'Blaming your father will only make you bitter. And I don't want you to be bitter!'

'I am not blaming him,' he exploded gruffly. 'I am blaming myself—*myself*!'

'But—none of it really matters now, don't you see?' she pleaded. 'I love you,' she added anxiously.

He sighed, his dark head jerking on the pillow. 'What are you, Sara?' he rasped in angry disbelief. 'Some kind of saint that you can forgive me the unforgivable? I de-nounced your love! Your trust! Your honesty! I even denounced our own child!'

'But you came back,' she said gently. 'Even believing all those things about me. You came back to me. You wanted to try again. I think you even forgave!'

'Forgave.' He bit the word out bitterly. 'How magnanimous of me. How—un-Sicilian! I forgave you for what?' he demanded. 'For being yourself? For remaining true to yourself despite what we Santinos did to you?' He round out another sigh. 'Well, I will tell you something,' he said grimly. 'It will be a long time before I will forgive myself.'

'Another vendetta—against yourself this time?' she mocked, and with a weary sigh sat up on her knees. 'I hope you've got them all logged on computer somewhere or you may lose track of who you are actually at war with!'

'I am not at war with you,' he said gruffly, his eyes beginning to burn again with that look which said that her angry pose aroused him.

And the fact that he had the arrogance to do that when they were in the middle of a serious discussion like this aroused her—to anger, bitter, biting anger. 'Well, I am at war with you!' she declared, tugging her robe around her to block out what his eyes were so greedily feeding on. 'And so long as you refuse to forgive both yourself and your father I refuse to forgive you!'

With that, she climbed off the bed.

'Was that an ultimatum?' he enquired.

'Yes.' Her wonderful hair flicked out as she turned to face him. 'I won't live with vendettas,' she snapped. 'If I can put my grievances aside then I don't see why you can't.'

'And have you?' he asked. 'Put your grievances aside?'

She looked down and away. 'Most of them,' she muttered. 'I can forgive Alfredo because he's old and sick and genuinely contrite. And I can forgive you because you were deliberately misled into believing what you did about me. But..'

'But?' he prompted softly when she stopped.

Yes, but, she thought, and lifted her chin to him. The blue eyes were cold, the lovely mouth tight. 'I saw you at the mayor's ball with Anastasia,' she said. 'I won't forgive you that, Nicolas. Not when you'd promised me she was out of the picture.'

'And what did you see?' He sat up, his frown cleverly giving the impression that he did not know what she was talking about.

'You, talking to her.' She turned away. 'Holding her. Kissing her.'

'Is that why you came home without me? Because what you saw hurt and upset you?'

She didn't answer, didn't need to; it was already written in the dull, throbbing silence.

'Did my father not try to explain to you about Anastasia?' he asked grimly after a moment.

She folded her arms across her chest because she was hurting inside again. 'He said I should ask you before I made judgements,' she murmured.

'And are you asking me now?'

She looked down at her feet and shook her head.

'Why not?'

She thought about that, and felt the tears sting her eyes again. 'Because I'm too frightened of the answer,' she confessed in a strained whisper.

He rolled off the bed, sighing heavily as he did so. 'As I was afraid of having blood tests taken of Lia,' he murmured. 'Because I was afraid of the answer.'

'You were?' That made her turn to look at him. He saw the tears and swore softly, reaching out to pull her against him, one hand pressing her face into his chest, the other circling her waist.

'Of course.' He grimaced. 'I wanted her to be mine so much, it was easier to simply—tell myself she was mine and leave it at that than learn the opposite.'

'She is yours,' she told him, just in case he had any doubts left in his mind.

He didn't. 'I know it,' he said. 'But Anastasia is not mine.' His eyes were dark with apology as she tipped back her head to look at him. 'Never was.' He lifted a finger to the corner of her quivering mouth. 'She belongs to Toni,' he added softly, then grimaced at her start of surprise. 'His future bride, to be exact. But since my father took ill Toni and I have been so busy that he has barely had time to be with her, never mind arrange a wedding. She is beautiful. She is kind. And she has a very sick mother—much the same as I have a sick father.' He shrugged. 'So if I am at home and Toni is not I have got into the habit of going to visit her a couple of times a week. To break her tedium. She does not get out much.'

'But she was out on the night of the mayor's ball.'

He sighed. 'And wanted to meet you. I would not let her,' he admitted. 'Because I had used her name to hurt you and did not want to hurt you more by introducing you to what, for you, amounted to my mistress. Anastasia was angry when I had to tell her why I did not want you both to meet, so we went outside while I apologised and did a little—begging.'

Another grimace. 'I promised her she could have Toni back for a whole month if she would just give me a few more weeks to cement my relationship with you. She agreed, on the condition that I also promised to tell you the truth about her—straight away. To which I agreed. Only the baby took ill,' he reminded her heavily. 'And my promise went right out of my head because I had too many other things to worry about, like how did I tell Sara that I loved our beautiful daughter when the child was lying there at death's door?'

His mouth tightened. 'Too late. I had left it too late to say all the things I wanted to say to both you and Lia. Then my father came in with his grand confession—' another rasping sigh '—and broke my whole world apart. After that, I did not feel I had the right to say anything to either you or Lia. I deserved neither of you.'

'So you went away to wage a vendetta against yourself?'

His endorsing smile was wry. 'Until I received that hysterical call from my father,' he said. 'Then I was back here as quick as my car would bring me.'

'If you forgive him, I'll forgive you for lying about Anastasia,' Sara offered.

'You are asking me to be very un-Sicilian again,' he sighed.

'You want more incentive?' Her blue eyes began to darken with promises. 'Only I have this—vision, you see,' she murmured softly, her fingers beginning to slowly undo the buttons on his shirt. 'Of a man lying naked on a bed of white linen with his woman lying on top of him, saying words that would—'

The hungry crush of his mouth caught the rest of what she had been going to say. 'You win,' he muttered. 'I am the most un-Sicilian person I know. I forgive everyone!' he announced. 'Even my father, though he does not deserve it!'

'Can I tell him that?' She smiled happily.

'Later.' He bent to lift her into his arms. 'The old devil can wait his turn! For we have a vision to play out before any more forgiving is done around here.'

'You're wearing too many clothes for my vision,' Sara complained.

'Now, yes,' he agreed. 'In a moment—no.' He dumped her on the bed and began dragging off his clothes while she watched him, her blue eyes hiding nothing as bronzed skin was exposed to her, bit by delicious bit.

'Will this do?' he enquired lazily when he was standing arrogantly naked in front of her.

'Pull the curtains,' she whispered sensually. 'Lock the doors and release the curtains around the bed.'

His eyes darkened, then blazed. He moved off like the graceful animal he was to do exactly what she had asked. As the fine white silk billowed around the bed, he was lying beside her, then beneath her, her robe gone, her hair around his shoulders, her arms braced on his wide chest, her eyes loving, solemnly loving.

'Beautiful,' she murmured. 'You're so beautiful, Nicolas . . .'

Harlequin Women Know Romance When They See It.

And they'll see it on **ROMANCE CLASSICS**, the new 24-hour TV channel devoted to romantic movies and original programs like the special **Romantically Speaking—Harlequin® Goes Prime Time.**

Romantically Speaking—Harlequin® Goes Prime Time introduces you to many of your favorite romance authors in a program developed exclusively for Harlequin® readers.

Watch for **Romantically Speaking—Harlequin® Goes Prime Time** beginning in the summer of 1997.

*If you're not receiving **ROMANCE CLASSICS**, call your local cable operator or satellite provider and ask for it today!*

Escape to the network of your dreams.

ROMANCE CLASSICS

HARLEQUIN ◆ PRESENTS ®

It may be cold outside—but inside a Harlequin Presents, the temperature's always rising! Get under the covers of these sizzling books from some of our hottest authors:

November 1997—**Gold Ring of Betrayal** (#1917)
Michelle Reid

Winner of the *Romantic Times* Reviewers' Choice Award for best Harlequin Presents 1994-95

December 1997—**Merry Christmas** (#1923)
Emma Darcy

Presents bestselling author with over 50 million books in print

January 1998—**A Marriage to Remember** (#1929)
Carole Mortimer

"Carole Mortimer delivers quality romance."
—*Romantic Times*

Warm up this winter with Harlequin Presents!

Available wherever Harlequin books are sold.

TA497

1998

Keep track of important dates

SUNDAY	MONDAY	TUESDAY	WEDNESDAY	THURSDAY	FRIDAY	SATURDAY

Three beautiful and colorful calendars that celebrate some of the most popular trends in America today.

Look for:

Just Babies—a 16 month calendar that features a full year of absolutely adorable babies!

Hometown Quilts
1998 Calendar

A 16 month quilting extravaganza!

Hometown Quilts—a 16 month calendar featuring quilted art squares, plus a short history on twelve different quilt patterns.

Inspirations—a 16 month calendar with inspiring pictures and quotations.

Value priced at $9.99 U.S./$11.99 CAN., these calendars make a perfect gift!

Available in retail outlets in August 1997.

Steeple Hill™

◆ HARLEQUIN®

CAL98

1998 CALENDAR
Just Babies
16 months of adorable bundles of joy

Inspirations
A 16 month calendar that will lift your spirits and gladden your heart

Look what Santa brought!

CHRISTMAS DELIVERY

Capture the holiday spirit with these three
heartwarming stories of moms, dads,
babies and mistletoe. *Christmas Delivery*
is the perfect stocking stuffer featuring three
of your favorite authors:

A CHRISTMAS MARRIAGE by Dallas Schulze
DEAR SANTA by Margaret St. George
THREE WAIFS AND A DADDY by Margot Dalton

There's always room for one more—
especially at Christmas!

Available wherever Harlequin and Silhouette
books are sold.

HARLEQUIN®   Silhouette®

Look us up on-line at: http://www.romance.net

HRE01197